The Adventures of CDL Mikey

T. J. Wray

ISBN- (paperback) 978-1-0878-1946-4

ASIN- (digital)- B081727NZP

A novel by T. J. Wray
First Edition

Contents

Chapter One
<u>Introduction</u>

This book is based on a real-life story. The names have been changed to protect the innocent. All of the characters in this book are a figment of my imagination. Any chance of these names existing in the real world is strictly coincidental. Since I don't have a big enough imagination to make up a book right out of thin air. This story is based on my real-life experiences. From the time in my life when I spent over twenty-five years driving commercial vehicles. After breaking my back at an early age. I was forced to find jobs that didn't require a lot of heavy lifting or manual labor. Therefore spending most of my life driving commercial vehicles for a living. If you enjoy Mikey's story please share it with someone you love.

=====================

Just as I have done in my other books. I would like to apologize upfront for my lack of command of the English language. I don't speak proper English and I'm not politically correct. I'm from Texas and I say Howdy, Y'all, and Ain't. Being from Texas makes English my second language. As (Texan) would be my first. So please forgive me. Thank you.

==================

Michael Van Winkle, (Mikey), is a CDL truck driver, who can legally drive anything with a steering wheel. He has a class (A), (CDL) commercial driver's license, with every endorsement the law will allow. He has a Hazmat endorsement, which means he can haul hazardous materials like gasoline and other flammable liquids. He has a double/triples and tanker endorsement. Which means he can haul two or three trailers at once. And he can haul things inside a tanker, like gas or milk or other liquids.

He also has a passenger endorsement. Which means he can drive anything with passengers. Like a trolley or transit bus, or even a school bus. He also drives heavy equipment like tractors and front end loaders. He can drive anything from a firetruck to a concrete mixer to a forklift. From a party bus to a dump truck.

He loves his job and he loves to drive. Mikey lives in Dallas Texas. And his job requires him to drive something different every day. He is a fill-in driver, who goes wherever he is needed and drives whatever they need him to drive. Mikey loves to drive. He loves his job and the thrill and adventure of getting to drive something different every day. And he loves going to new places every day. He also loves all the people he gets to meet on his many jobs.

He works for a driver consultant company called (Part-Time Driver). Who dispatches him to a different job site every day. He has driven everything from a taxi cab to an 18-wheeler during his twelve years with the company. The owner of Part-Time Driver is a man named Ted Mulberry. Ted Knows he can count on Mikey to always do a good job. He knows Mikey is an honest, hardworking man who will do the job right the first time.

Mikey also works as a fill-in firetruck driver and a volunteer firefighter. Anytime they need him at the firehouse, he drops everything and goes running as fast as he can. Also, he is the biggest (Dallas Cowboys) football fan on the planet. He never misses watching a game and goes to as many as he can. He has never been married and has no children. Even though he loves kids, he has never met the right woman yet.

Mikey is a God-fearing man and goes to church every Sunday morning. In his free time, he does a lot of volunteer work around his church. Like yard work and maintenance. He attends the First Baptist Church of Dallas.

==================

Mikey was born in Dallas Texas in 1961. His parents named him Michael, but he has been Mikey from day one. He grew up on the north side of Dallas in the '60s and '70s. When (The Beatles), and (The Rolling Stones), were popular. And real men were still cowboys.

He was an only child, his parents had raised him right though. He was always very close to his parents, especially his mother. She took him everywhere she went when he was small. His dad taught him the love of fishing at an early age. He learned to throw a football and bat a baseball from his dad. But he got his love of people from his mother. She was very active in her church, she was on the PTA at Mikey's school. And a school teacher at his school. She was a social butterfly and taught Mikey the same.

His father (Berry) had grown up in the 1930s and '40s in southern Oklahoma. After the dust bowl and the great depression. He came from a farming family. But moved to the Austin area by 1950 to attend Texas A&M college. Where he met his bride (Martha), and they were married in 1953. Martha was a Science major at A&M, Berry was there on a football scholarship. But he blew out his knee and only played half a season before they met.

Martha came from back east where her parents ran a shoe store. They sent her to Texas to go to university, thinking she would meet a nice southern man. After they were married they settled in north Dallas. Where Berry worked as an accountant. And Martha worked as a school teacher.

When Mikey came along in '61, they were already well established in their community as well as in their church. They both volunteered at their church and helped with youth outings. They both loved children and had been trying to have a child of their own for many years. They thought there was something wrong with them because, after seven years of marriage, they still weren't pregnant.

They prayed almost daily that God would bless them with a child. Then a miracle happened. Well at least in their minds it was a miracle. In the summer of 1960, Martha got pregnant. The Van Winkles were the happiest couple on the block. The pregnancy brought them closer together than they had ever been before.

Berry was already an awesome husband. But once Martha got pregnant, he did everything for her. He even went to lamas classes with her. When the doctor told them it was going to be a boy, they were very excited. They told all of their friends and everyone at church. They threw the biggest baby shower Dallas Texas had ever seen. There were probably 300 people there.

Mikey grew up going to church and by the time he was a teenager, he was a man of God. He played football just as his father had, from the time he could walk. He and his dad did a lot of fishing in his early years. His dad owned a small fishing boat that they kept in the marina at Lewisville Lake just north of Dallas. In Mikey's memory, it seemed they went fishing every weekend between the age of three and thirteen.

By the time Mikey was a teenager, he was so involved with football, there wasn't much time for fishing. By high school, he was on the varsity team. He even got a scholarship because of his football skills.

Mikey fell in love with a beautiful blond girl in high school. But she wanted to be a doctor and ended up leaving Dallas after high school to pursue that career. He was heartbroken, but he knew life must go on. They remained friends for many years and became penpals. Mikey even kept track of her career. Years later she became a well-known doctor in Pennsylvania.

After high school, Mikey planned to go to college at Texas A&M. Where his parents had gone, and where they met.

Chapter Two
<u>The Fire</u>

Today Mikey is filling in at a tire factory. Where he will be driving a giant forklift all day, and loading tires from the dock of the factory into trucks. He gets there early because he hasn't driven a forklift in awhile, and wants to familiarize himself with the controls. He has been practicing picking up tires with the giant forklift for about 45 minutes. He quickly realizes this forklift is very powerful and could pick up the whole world, it seems. It picks up thousands of pounds with ease. Then suddenly his pager goes off with (911). It's the fire department!

You see Mikey is also the fill-in firetruck driver and a volunteer firefighter. And anytime there is a fire and they need a truck driver, they call him immediately. He has to drop everything and go to the fire station as quickly as possible. Anytime his pager says 911, he runs to the fire station as fast as he can go.

There was a huge house fire on the other side of town. Mikey jumped off of the forklift and went to the fire station as fast as he could go. By the time they got to the fire, the house was totally engulfed in flames. Luckily everyone had already gotten out of the house, except the family dog.

While the other firemen were unwrapping their hoses. Mikey ran in the back door of the house and grabbed the dog (Sparky), just in the nick of time. Sparky was slightly singed and scared but turned out to be just fine. Mikey laughed. He thought Sparky was a fitting name for a dog who had just been saved from a house fire.

Everyone said Mikey was a hero. But he said he was just doing his job, and he was glad he could help. After the fire was out, Mikey went back to the tire warehouse and spent the day loading tires. He had a big smile on his face all day long. He really loved helping people.

He learned a lot that day about stacking tires. He found out the hard way that you can't just stack them in vertical rows or they will fall over. You have to overlap each tire so they will stay in place. But all in all, he felt like it had been a good day. After all, he did save someone's pet dog. And he met some nice people at his job site. He really loved helping people. He really loved his job. It had been a great day.

=====================

At the end of the day, after he had clocked out. Mikey headed back to his car. As he walked past a small s-10 Chevy Blazer, he noticed someone sleeping in the back seat. He thought that was odd. Someone sleeping that time of day in their car. Plus, as cold as it was outside that day, he was worried that they might be freezing cold.

He walked on by reluctant to bother them. Then something inside him told him to go back and check on them. He walked back and knocked on the side window of the Blazer, but the guy didn't move. So he knocked a little harder and yelled "Hey" this time. Still, the guy didn't move. Mikey pulled open the door and yelled at the guy to wake up!

As soon as he opened the door, he knew something was terribly wrong. The horrible smell just about knocked him down.

Mikey yelled again, but in the back of his mind, he knew the guy was already dead.

Mikey ran back inside and called 911. He had to stay and fill out the police report since he was the one who found the body. It turned out the guy was homeless and had crawled into the first car he could find that was unlocked. Just to get out of the cold and get some sleep. He had a pan of charcoal that he had lit to keep warm. The police said, with all the windows rolled up in the car. It looked like he had gone to sleep and suffocated from the fumes. Then he just never woke up again.

Mikey felt so bad, he had never seen a dead person before. He had spent several years in the military but had never shot at anyone or been shot at. He wasn't on the front lines. He was a truck driver. He never saw any real live action. He felt so bad for this poor guy and his family. He hadn't really thought about it before. But where do homeless people go when it gets cold outside?

As Mikey drove home, he wondered if there was anything he could do to help the homeless in his neighborhood. He thought he would go and talk to his pastor and the people in his church.

The following Sunday Mikey got up and spoke to his church congregation about the poor dead guy he had found in the car. With a heavy heart, he asked if there was anything he could do to help out the freezing homeless people. After a lot of talk and input from everyone. They decided to put up a sign in front of the church. Saying that the church would be open 24 hours a day, on cold days. If anyone was looking for a place to get warm. They would be welcome to come inside.

Mikey was glad he had decided to talk with his church. He was also glad they were leaving the doors open on cold days. But he still thought there must be more he could do to help. Like volunteering at a soup kitchen or having a church coat drive for the homeless. He would definitely put more thought into it in the future. He thought we should all do a little more to help solve the homeless crisis...

Chapter Three
<u>Vandalized Truck</u>

Today Mikey was called in to drive a Big Hook wrecker for O'Malley's Towing Service. This is one of those giant tow trucks you see hauling other big trucks around. Towing semi-trailers and 18 wheelers.

When he got to the main office, the supervisor (Joe), told him he would be driving truck number 318 today. Then Joe gave Mikey $200 and told him he would need to fuel the truck up at some point during the day. Mikey went out to the yard and found truck #318. It was a beautiful Peterbilt, and it looked brand new. It was a beautiful sky blue color, it had all the bells and whistles. It had a beautiful two-tone pinstriping going down both sides that almost looked like clouds. Mikey smiled, thinking to himself, it is going to be a great day today. What a beautiful truck.

The first thing he did was to complete his pre-driving inspection, that he always did on every vehicle before he drove it. He checked all the fluid levels and kicked all the tires. He then made sure all the lights and signals worked properly. Then he checked the toolboxes that were mounted on both sides of the truck. There were jacks and lug wrenches, and every hand tool you could imagine in those toolboxes. Mikey was impressed with this truck, to say the least. He thought the guy who normally drives this magnificent truck is a lucky fella.

Then Mikey climbed up into the cab and fired it up. It sounded awesome with its big diesel engine purring. Just then Mikey noticed a shotgun hanging in the rear window. He thought maybe it's just for looks, or to scare away would-be criminals. Then he looked under the seat and found a billy club. Then he looked into the glove box and there were a handgun and two boxes of shells. Mikey thought, man this guy is loaded for bear. He must be expecting trouble. Mikey put the $200 fuel money under the sun visor.

Then he went back inside and asked supervisor Joe, why were there so many guns in this truck. The supervisor said that Jim, the guy who normally drives that truck, was once mugged and robbed. While he was out on a call picking up a broken-down truck. So nowadays Jim always carries a gun with him, just in case. Mikey said, "Well guns scare me, so I'll just leave them alone and act like they aren't even there". Then supervisor Joe said, "Okay, be careful out there and have a good day". Mikey said, "Thank you, you too boss".

Then Mikey went back out and climbed up into the giant tow truck. He turned on the CB radio and did his radio check. He said, "Breaker-Breaker, for a radio check". The dispatcher said, "It's working, your checks in the mail". He said, "Your first call is to go out on I-35 and pick up a broken down 18-wheeler. It's at mile marker 458 and It's in the north-bound lane. It is an orange and white Schneider Truck".

Mikey said, "Ten-Four", and headed out onto the highway to try out this brand new Big Hook Wrecker he was driving. He found the broken-down truck and thirty minutes later had it all hooked up. With hooks, safety chains, and lights all in place. He had a big smile on his face the whole time he was hooking up that broken-down truck.

From where he was parked he had the prettiest view of Lewisville Lake, on the north side of Dallas. And it reminded him of his father. One of Mikey's favorite things to do in his spare time was to go fishing. He liked fishing almost as much as he liked driving. His father had taught him how to fish when he was young. And any chance he got he would go fishing and usually take one of the neighbor kids with him.

After hooking up all of his tow lights he headed for the mechanic shop where he was supposed to take the broken-down truck. Mikey was really impressed with the enormous power of this giant tow truck. He thought you could tow anything with this super powerful truck.

It was hard to turn corners though. He was towing a semi-truck that was almost 75 feet long on its own. Then his Big Hook Wrecker was about 35 feet long on its own. So together they were close to 115 feet long. This makes it extremely hard to turn a corner. You have to swing as wide as possible and watch everything in your path.

Like curbs and telephone poles and of course all the traffic.

The trip took twice as long as normal because of the slow turning and all-around slow-moving. He made it to the mechanic shop without incident and dropped the broken down Scheider truck inside their yard. Then he figured he better go to the truckstop and fuel up his truck because the tanks were both well below a quarter of a tank. After grabbing his paperwork he headed out.

Just as he was pulling out of the mechanic yard and back out onto the street. A speeding car came flying around the corner. Mikey didn't see it until it was too late. The car was absolutely speeding down the road. The speeding car caught its right side back bumper on the front left side of Mikey's truck's front bumper. Just as he was pulling out onto the road. It all happened really quickly and startled Mikey. He didn't even have time to react. The speeding car didn't even stop, or slow down much. It just kept on speeding away, and disappeared around the corner, out of sight.

Mikey hit the parking brake and jumped out to assess the damage. The front bumper of this brand new truck was bent sideways and all crumpled up to one side. Mikey just froze in terror, he couldn't believe his eyes. He backed the truck up and ran back into the mechanic shop. Two or three mechanics were standing at the shops open bay doors. They had been watching the whole wreck unfold. They heard the screeching tire sound and metal crashing sounds and came running to the doorway to check it out.

Mikey said, "Did you see that guy? He just ran into me and drove off". One of the mechanics said, "Yeah, I recognize that kid. I think he works around the corner at that auto salvage yard over there". So Mikey quickly jumped back into his truck and took off towards the salvage yard around the corner.

Sure enough, the old green Oldsmobile with the bent rear bumper. Which had just run over him, was parked right in front of the office. Mikey found a spot to park his Big Truck and went inside the office. The guy in the office said, "The kid that drives that car isn't here. I sent him on an errand." He said, "You can fill out an incident report while you wait If you want to". Then he handed Mikey a piece of paper and a pencil. Mikey wasn't sure what to do. So he set down to fill out the report, while he waited.

About 15 minutes passed, and a young man about 18 years old walked through the door. Mikey quickly recognized the kid as the guy who was driving the car that had hit his truck. Mikey jumped to his feet and said, "Hey you're the guy who hit my truck a while ago and just drove off". The kid said, "I was late for work and in a hurry. Besides, no one seemed to be hurt anyway". Mikey said, "You damaged my truck, let's go outside and I'll show you the damage".

As they walked outside Mikey could see the driver's door of his truck was standing wide open. He said out loud, "Oh my God!, I forgot to lock the doors on my truck". He immediately ran to the truck. He could see there was a problem. The first thing he noticed was the shotgun was no longer hanging in the rear window. Then he thought, Oh my God again. The $200 under the sun visor. Yep, it was also gone.

Then he noticed the billy club and all the tie-down straps, that had been under the seat, were also missing. He jumped into the cab and opened the glove box, "Oh my God"! He cried, a third time. The handgun and all the ammo was also gone. Then he jumped down and started tearing open all the toolboxes on the sides of the truck. They were also all empty. All the jacks and wrenches and hand tools were all gone too. Even all the chains and hooks and bungee cords, that hung on the back headache rack, were all missing.

Someone had stolen everything on that truck that wasn't bolted down. Mikey was sick with grief, and almost in tears. He reached for the CB radio, to call his dispatcher. Just then he realized, even the CB radio had been taken. They even took the (tow lights) that were magnetically stuck on the rear of the truck. Mikey was so sick he felt like throwing up. He walked back inside, with the kid, and asked the guy at the desk if he could use his telephone. Mikey used the phone to call the police department. Then, through his tears, he called supervisor Joe and tried to explain what had happened.

When the police arrived on the scene, Mikey told them the whole story. From the beginning where the boy had hit his truck around the corner and then just kept on driving. Then he filled out a police report on everything that was missing from his truck, as well as he could. He wasn't really positive about the tools because he didn't know what all was in there, to begin with.

By this time there was already a detective on the scene, who had been assigned to the case. Because of the missing guns and ammo. Detective Mike Williams was on the case. Mikey had been at this auto salvage yard for almost two hours. Filling out paperwork and telling his story to Detective Williams.

Just then Mikey saw a group of 5 or 6 young men walking by. They looked to be teenagers. Mikey asked detective Williams if he knew any of the boys. Detective Williams said he recognized the older looking one, as a leader of a gang of thugs who lived in a trailer park a few blocks away. Detective

Williams said, "That tall one is Magill. And he's the leader of the group. They stay in trouble and he's been arrested many times". Mikey said, "I wonder if they know anything about my stolen stuff"? Detective Williams said, "I don't know, but let's ask 'em".

Detective Williams then called the boys over and asked them if they knew anything, or had seen anything of the stolen tools and guns. He told them it was a very serious crime and if they knew anything at all, they better speak-up immediately. The boys all denied knowing anything, or even seeing anything.

Magill did most of the talking. He said, "We ain't seen nothing cop! If we do, we'll give you a call". Then he just laughed and turned around and walked off. Detective Williams said, "They probably did it, or at least know something about it. But they will never talk to the police, and we don't have any evidence against them at this time". Mikey was sad and dropped his head, knowing the stuff would probably never be recovered.

Then the detective and Mikey went back inside the salvage yard office to question the owner and the kid. They said there were no security cameras on the property and they had lots of stuff stolen in the past.

Mikey then drove his crumpled up truck back to O'Malley's Towing Service, where his day had started. He felt so terrible. He could hardly talk as he told the entire story to Joe and gave him a copy of the police report. Then Mikey and supervisor Joe went outside and looked at the bent up front bumper of the truck. Which had looked so magnificent just a few hours earlier.

Mikey showed the supervisor the hole in the dash, where the CB radio used to be. Then he opened all the toolboxes, which were empty. Then he opened the glove box and showed the supervisor that the guns and ammo were also missing. He said he had put the $200 fuel money under the sun visor and it was also missing. Mikey was just sickened by the whole day's events. He felt so bad, he just wanted to go home and forget this day ever happened. Just then, he remembered thinking that morning, that it was going to be a great day. It had turned out to be the worst day of his life.

Joe said they had insurance that would cover the repairs to the front of the truck and replace the stolen tools and hooks and chains. But Mikey would be responsible for replacing the guns and ammo. As well as the $200 in cash, that was taken from the sun visor. Mikey was just about in tears. He turned to the supervisor and said, "It's all my fault Joe, and I will pay you back for everything, I promise".

Now you have to understand. Mikey considered himself to be an honest man. He had always treated people the way he wanted to be treated. Just like the good book says. Mikey had always tried to do the right thing, in every situation. At the age of only 36, Mikey was debt-free. His house was paid for and he didn't owe a dime to anyone. Even though most of his jobs barely paid much more than minimum wage. He had always been able to stay out of debt.

The problem was, he didn't have any money in savings. Because it took everything he made just to survive. So Mikey wasn't sure how in the world he was going to be able to pay supervisor Joe for all the things that had gone wrong on this day.

The following day supervisor Joe called Mikey to give him the bad news. Joe said it was going to cost $2500 to replace the front bumper of the truck. And almost $8000 to replace all the tools, chains and hooks that were stolen. Then another $400 for a new CB radio, and about $700 for the guns and ammo. Plus the $200 in cash that was under the sun visor. All total, it would cost Mikey $11,800 for the damages to the truck.

Mikey couldn't believe his ears. He couldn't believe someone could do that much damage to his truck in just the few short minutes he was away from it. He thought that even at $200 or $300 a month, it would take him years to pay back that much money. But he still promised Joe that he would somehow, pay back every penny for the damages that he felt solely responsible for. Mikey was thinking he would just have to work extra shifts for the next two or three years and give the money to Joe.

Even though it was a terrible situation, Mikey felt if he worked hard, he would get through it. Mikey knew the insurance would have paid for most of the damages. But he felt so bad that he was responsible for such terrible damage to such a nice truck. He felt in his heart that he should pay the company back for everything that was lost.

Mikey was so upset after hearing all that bad news from supervisor Joe, that he couldn't sleep a wink that night. The next morning he thought that maybe if he went down to the trailer park and found Magill. He could talk to Magill and get some answers. Or at least, he thought he could look around.

So, Mikey drove down to the trailer park. He could not believe what he saw. The conditions were deplorable. He couldn't believe that people could live like that. Not even in the projects or slums. There was a broken sign at the entrance that said (Taylors Trailer Park). Someone had handwritten (Enter at your own Risk). The trailer houses were all run down and falling apart. Some had even fallen completely down.

The yards were all unkempt, and the grass was waist-high in some places. There was trash everywhere. There were a lot of old broken down cars, broken bicycles, and junk appliances scattered out everywhere. This was the worst place, that you could call home, that Mikey had ever seen.

He saw a little boy walking down the road and stopped and asked him if he knew a guy named Magill. The little boy said, "Yeah, he's bad and my mom won't allow me to talk to him". Then Mikey drove on into the trailer park deeper. He saw a group of about fifteen teenagers huddled around some old junk cars, with music playing very loudly.

Three or four of the kids walked up to Mikey's car. One of them said, "What do you want white boy"? Mikey said, "I'm looking for Magill". He turned and yelled "Gill!". Just then the tall guy that Mikey had seen the day before, emerged from the crowd. Mikey was scared and didn't dare get out of his car. Magill walked up and said, "What the hell do you want"? Mikey said, "Man, the damage to that truck yesterday is going to cost me nearly $12,000. If you know anything about it please tell me, and maybe I can recover some of the stuff that was stolen".

Magill furrowed his brow and said, "What do I look like to you, some kind of newspaper reporter? I don't have any information for you! You should have never come in here". He pulled out a switchblade knife. Looked Mikey right in the eyes and said, "If it wasn't the middle of the day, you'd be lucky to get out of here with your head still in tack! This place is for vato's only, white boy".

Just then he made a motion to the crowd and all the other guys came running over. Mikey was scared to death. He shoved his car into gear and took off with a screeching of his tires. He could see all those kids running after him, in his rearview mirror. When he got home he was still shaking from the whole traumatic experience.

Mikey finally decides to just chalk it up as a total loss on his part. Holding out hope that the police would eventually find some of the stolen stuff. In the meantime, he would just have to make the monthly payments to supervisor Joe. He knew one thing for sure though. He was never going back to that trailer park, as long as he lived. And he hoped he never ran into Magill again, ever. That guy scared the heck out of him.

Chapter Four
<u>The Big Game</u>

Today, Mikey is driving a church bus full of people to a Dallas Cowboys football game. It's Sunday morning and Mikey gets up early to go to Sunday school. He is very excited because he knows today is the Big Game. Between his beloved Dallas Cowboys and the Kansas City Chiefs.

Mikey goes to church and enjoys the service that morning. After Sunday School he heads out behind the church to fire up the bus and do his pre-trip inspection. He has been thinking all morning that he can't wait to get to the stadium. He is the world's biggest Dallas Cowboy fan and there is nothing he would rather do on a Sunday afternoon than going to Cowboy stadium for a football game.

Mikey has been to a lot of Cowboy games over the years and has many fond memories there. He once took his neighbor's little boy. The joy in little Randel's face made Mikey's day. They really enjoyed themselves. Even though

Dallas had lost that game. Mikey and little Randel had the time of their lives. Cheering on their team and eating popcorn and hot dogs.

Today's game doesn't start until 3 p.m., but Mikey wants to get there early because of the giant crowds. He will need a little extra time and room to park the church bus. So he gets everyone loaded onto the bus at about 12:30 and heads out to the stadium. It will take Mikey about 30 minutes to drive out to Arlington Texas where Cowboys stadium is at.

The closer he gets, the more excited Mikey gets. The Kansas City Chiefs have a good record this year. But Mikey knows the Cowboys have a good team and should win today's game. At least on paper, they should.

Upon arrival at the stadium, it takes a good 20 minutes to find a parking space for the bus. The crowd is already enormous. With all the tailgaters and partiers, the parking area is already packed with people. But he finally finds a good space and they head in to find their seats.

Dallas wins the coin toss and defers. So KC gets the ball first. At the opening kickoff, the crowd is going crazy. The entire stadium is rocking like an earthquake just hit it. Mikey loves the excitement and feeds off of the crowd. He is literally jumping with joy.

Kansas City drives down and scores an opening field goal to go up by three points. Now it's Dallas's turn. With one of the top-rated quarterbacks in the NFL (Troy Aikman), they don't have much trouble with Kansas City's defense. Dallas's Emmitt Smith scores an opening touchdown on their very first drive. Seven to three, Mikey is ecstatic. What a game! He looks over and notices the whole church crowd just going nuts, cheering for the team, after the touchdown.

The rest of the first half was pretty uneventful. Just a bunch of dead-end drives, followed by a lot of punts. But Mikey is still having an absolute blast. He would rather be right here right now than any other place he can think of. At the half-time break. Mikey and a couple of others go and get drinks for the entire church group. The weather is absolutely beautiful today. And other than fighting the massive crowd, you couldn't ask for a better day.

During the second half, the Dallas Cowboys go wild and run away with the game. Winning over Kansas City by 21 points. By the time the game is over Mikey's voice is completely hoarse from all the screaming and cheering on his team. What an absolutely glorious day. His entire body was smiling as they fought the crowd going back to the bus. There was nothing better than going to a Cowboys game on a Sunday afternoon. Plus his team winning just made it that much sweeter. And Mikey was getting paid to drive the bus. He couldn't ask for more. He really loved his job. And the people he got to work with. What a day! What a job.

Chapter Five
<u>The Pool</u>

Today Mikey is filling in as a concrete delivery truck driver for Mccormick Ready Mix. Or a mixer driver, as truck drivers call it. He has never driven a mixer before. But it is a Mack truck and he is very familiar with this type of rig. Today will be a learning experience, to say the least. Mikey is a great truck driver, but he knows very little about concrete. He finds out very early in the morning. That with the drum turning and all that concrete mixing around as you are driving, the truck handles and drives much differently than he had expected. Plus there is a huge learning curve as Mikey learns all about how to mix concrete.

As a mixer driver, you are responsible for getting the right mixture from the mixing plant. You have to look into the drum of your truck (as it's turning), and tell the plant operator if the slump and mixture are right. You do this by looking into the drum as it is mixing and then telling the plant operator if you think your load needs more concrete to make it thicker or more water to make it thinner. Because the plant operator can't see inside your drum. He is just guesstimating the mixture.

The (slump) of concrete is the thickness of the mixture. Also, Mikey had to learn that there are lots of ingredients in concrete. Like sand and gravel, and concrete dust. Then there are lots of additives like fiber to make the concrete stronger and different colorings to make the concrete a certain color that the customer may have asked for. So today was going to be a big learning experience for Mikey, to say the least.

Mikey's first load from the mixing plant was a blue colored load of concrete going to a new swimming pool that was being poured in a nearby neighborhood. Mikey learned quickly that it is better to leave the mixing plant with the concrete too thick, than with it too thin. There are water tanks on both sides of the truck. You can always add water to the mixture at the job site and make the concrete thinner. But if you leave the mixing plant with your load to thin, you cannot thicken it at the job site.

Because you have no way of taking water out, or you have no way of adding more concrete dust to thicken the load. So you have to be careful at the mixing plant and make sure you always leave the plant with your load just a little dry. Then you can add water at the job site if necessary.

Mikey got his first load just the way he wanted it at the mixing plant and took off to the swimming pool job site. Mikey had never seen a more organized job site. The foreman had everything in the right place. All the concrete forms were set and ready to go. All the workers were waiting and ready when he arrived with the first load of concrete.

Mikey backed his truck in and set up all his chutes. Then they had Mikey pour out a sample of the concrete, to make sure the slump was set just as they needed it to be. The foreman liked the thickness of the concrete and Mikey continued pouring. As the concrete poured out of his truck. Mikey thought it was one of the most beautiful things he had ever seen. Mikey had never seen (blue) concrete poured before. He thought this swimming pool would be awesome when it was finished.

The concrete mixer could only carry nine yards of concrete at a time. They were going to need about 35 yards of concrete to finish this swimming pool. So Mikey had to make four trips back and forth between the mixing plant and the swimming pool job site. These four trips took Mikey the entire day, not counting a 30-minute lunch break.

The swimming pool was completed and absolutely beautiful by quitting time. Mikey was very proud. Not only of a job well done, but also proud of all the new things he had learned and experienced about the concrete business. After watching all those concrete workers working their butts off all day. Mikey was glad he was just the delivery guy and not a concrete finisher. He thought those guys have a really hard job. They have to work out in the heat all day and it is all very tough manual labor. He thought they really have a hard job.

Mikey rinsed the drum of his truck out and cleaned all of his tools and chutes up and put them away for the day. He had a big smile on his face as he headed back to the Mccormick Ready Mix yard to park his truck. What an experience, what a day he thought. He looked forward to the next time he would get to drive a concrete mixer. He felt pride in a job well done…

=====================

Mikey didn't know it, but he would end up spending the next two days at Mccormick Ready Mix also. Ted at Part-Time Driver, told him to just keep working there for three days in a row. Because Mr. Mccormick had been very short-handed lately and needed the help.

Over the next two days, Mikey would become an almost expert mixer driver. He poured concrete all over the northern Dallas metro area. He poured pads at new home sights. He poured concrete for sidewalks and curbs. He even poured concrete onto a new runway they were building at the Air National Guard airstrip.

By the end of the three day period, Mikey felt very comfortable with the concrete business. He thought he could now drive a mixer in the future without even thinking about it twice. He shook Mr. Mccormick's hand and thanked him for the experience. Mr. Mccormick said, "Thank you, son, I'm sure we will need you again in the near future. It seems like it's hard to keep good drivers around". Mikey really liked Mr. Mccormick and looked forward to helping him out again someday.

Chapter Six
<u>The Federal Building</u>

Today Mikey will be driving a busload of people from Dallas Texas, to Oklahoma City. It is his local Baptist Church's choir group. 55 people are going on the trip and Mikey is going to drive their church bus to Oklahoma City. They are going to visit the Alfred P. Murrah federal building bombing site, and the National Memorial and Museum there. Then they are going to visit the Oklahoma City Zoo. Then they will be driving back home late that evening.

Mikey has to get up very early today. His bus trip is scheduled to leave at five a.m. Mikey gets up at four and takes a shower and eats his breakfast. Then he heads down to the church to get his bus keys and start his pre-trip inspection on the bus. First, he checks the tires and all the lights. Then he pops the hood and checks all the fluid levels. Then he fires the bus up and checks the horn and windshield wipers.

Then he makes sure the spare tire and lug wrench are there. Then he checks the fuel gauge and it shows full. Mikey learned a long time ago, it's always better to be safe than sorry. So he is very meticulous about his pre-trip inspection. Then he makes sure the air conditioner is working properly. It's going to be a long hot summer day and Mikey wants his guests to be comfortable.

Then he pulls the bus around to the front of the church and starts loading up all his passengers. They all have day bags but there really isn't much luggage. They have two big ice chest full of bottled drinking water. Mikey puts the two chests in through the back door of the bus. He slides them over to one side to not block the emergency door exit. Then he climbs into the driver's seat and thanked everyone for coming. He tells them to just relax and enjoy the trip. Then north up the highway, they go.

It will take about three and a half hours to drive to Oklahoma City. They are planning to stop about halfway and get fuel and something to eat. The first part of the trip is uneventful except for when Mikey drives by a lady trying to change a flat tire. He pulls over when he notices she is all by herself. Mikey and a couple of the elderly gentlemen on the bus changed the flat tire for the lady and got her going. It was out in the middle of nowhere and a bad place for a lady to be alone. She tried to pay Mikey but he said, "No thanks, have a nice day". And they were back on the road.

About an hour later they stopped at a Love's truckstop and got fuel and some donuts. Everyone got out and stretched their legs. Mikey checked the tires on the bus. Everything was looking good. He went inside after fueling the bus and got a cup of coffee. The passengers on the bus offered Mikey a donut, which he gladly accepted. Then they headed north up I-35, towards Oklahoma City. Mikey enjoyed driving the bus. It was almost brand new and had all the bells and whistles. He used the cruise control on almost the entire trip. It was a very comfortable ride and easy to drive.

They arrived in Oklahoma City at about 9 a.m. There was a lot of traffic but Mikey didn't have much trouble finding the Murrah building memorial site. He pulled up to the front door and started unloading his passengers. Usually, on these types of trips, Mikey always stayed on the bus. He would have normally found a parking place for a large bus and just stayed with the bus until the people came out and were ready to go. But not today! Mikey had wanted to visit the Oklahoma City bombing memorial ever since it happened in 1995. And today he was going to get his chance.

After everyone was off the bus Mikey pulled around the block and parked the bus under a shade tree. He locked the bus up and put the keys in his pocket. Then he ran as fast as he could to catch up with the church tour group. He didn't want to miss a word the tour guide said.

The guide talked about Timothy McVeigh and Terry Nichols. And how it was the worst domestic terrorist attack in American history. She said a moving truck full of fertilizer based explosives was parked in front of the building. When it blew up it took out one whole side of the building. She said 168 people died that day, 19 of which were children that were in a daycare center inside the Murrah Federal Building.

Mikey was so sad as he listened to the story. The guide talked about the heroic first responders who risked life and limb to try and pull people from the rubble. When the tour guide said Timothy McVeigh was arrested 90 minutes after the explosion by a state trooper, everyone in the church group clapped their hands.

Then the tour guide talked for 20 minutes about what she called the (Oklahoma Standard). She said that after the bombing, and a brief morning period. The people of Oklahoma pulled together and vowed to rebuild their city and their hearts. And they did. They first built the memorial site and then the museum to the Alfred P. Murrah Federal Building.

Today the Oklahoma Standard is still going strong. And Oklahoma City just keeps getting stronger. After the tour, Mikey felt closer to the people of Oklahoma City than he had ever felt before. He was glad he decided to park the bus and take the tour. It was an eye-opening experience for sure. Practically the entire group was in tears as they exited the memorial.

After the tour of the Murrah building.

They left the bus parked and walked over two or three blocks and ate lunch at a BBQ place. Again Mikey didn't usually eat with people he took on bus trips because he didn't really know any of them. But today he decided to eat lunch with them, since they had invited him to, and it was his church group. He felt really close to this group after the Murrah building tour. Several of the ladies in the group had even hugged him when they saw tears in his eyes at the Murrah building. They had a nice lunch, then walked back to the bus.

Mikey decided to zig-zag through downtown as they were headed to the northeast side of town to look for the Oklahoma City Zoo. He figured if he zig-zagged and took the long way, they would have a chance to see the city a little bit. After driving around for about 30 minutes he finally found the zoo. They asked him to join them in visiting the zoo. But Mikey said. "No thanks. I think I will set this one out and just stay with the bus".

He unloaded all his passengers at the front gate and went and found a nice parking place for the bus. He parked way back in the back of the parking lot, out of everybody's way. The group ended up staying in the zoo for almost 3 hours. Mikey decided to take a nap while waiting. He stretched out across the aisle and went to sleep lying across two seats on the bus. He had never been to the Oklahoma City Zoo and didn't realize it was that big.

Finally, they all came out and got back on the bus. Mikey had turned the bus off most of the time they were gone. But he had fired it up about 30 minutes before they got back to cool it down with the air conditioner. It was really hot out that day.

Just before they took off. One of the elders got up and thanked everyone for coming and talked a little about what a great time they had that day. He even thanked Mikey for driving them and everyone gave him a big round of applause. Mikey had a big smile on his face as he headed down the highway.

All the way back to Dallas Mikey was thinking "What a job". He couldn't believe someone would pay him to drive around and have fun all day. Mikey loved to drive and he really loved his job. And the people he worked with were great. Mikey thought the Oklahoma City trip was one of the best trips he had ever been on. He really enjoyed himself and planned to come back one day.

Chapter Seven
Road Trip

Today Mikey is driving an 18-wheeler loaded with car parts for the Ford Motor Company. He has to take the load from Dallas Texas, to a drop yard in Wheeling West Virginia. Where he will drop his trailer full of car parts and pick up a trailer full of bottled water and bring it back to Walmart in Dallas Texas. All total this trip should take him about four days. He will take state highway 75 north out of Texas, and up through Oklahoma to I-40. Then go east through Arkansas, Tennessee and into Virginia. Then go north into West Virginia and up to Wheeling.

Luckily it's still summertime. Mikey knows from experience, some of those northern highways can be very treacherous to navigate in the wintertime. He doesn't have to worry too much about snowy roads. Living in Dallas it's not usually a problem. He really enjoys these occasional long road trips. It gives him a lot of time to think. And puts his whole life in perspective. Plus he gets to see some wondrous new places he has never seen before. Mikey thinks there is nothing like a road trip in the summertime on the great American roadways.

Early that morning Mikey picks up his truck and trailer at Carmichaels Trucking just north of Dallas. After collecting his paperwork and filling out his logbook. He checks the lock on the back door of his trailer and kicks all the tires. After checking all the lights, he fires up the big diesel engine and heads north on Highway 75. It is a beautiful sunny day, and Mikey is thinking it's going to be another great day.

The trip up to Oklahoma is fairly uneventful. He stops for lunch about halfway to I-40 and has a famous Oklahoma buffalo burger. Mikey had never eaten buffalo before. But he enjoys it and thinks it isn't much different than beef. He had always heard it was good, now he could recommend it to his friends. Then he continues up to I-40 and turns east. So far, so good. He's making pretty good time. He doesn't want to be late with his load. So he keeps the truck moving.

Mikey's father had always taught him not to get in a big hurry when driving on a long road trip. His dad said, "Just keep the wheels turning. Slow and steady always wins the race". So Mikey always tries to drive the speed limit and not get in too big of a hurry. Safe and steady.

He spends a lot of time on this trip thinking about Magill and wondering how someone so young could get so mean and hateful. He wonders if there is anything he could do to help. Maybe he could volunteer to clean up the trailer park or do some mowing out there. Maybe he could get some of the teenagers to pitch in and help him haul off all those junk cars and scrap metal. They could use the money from the scrap metal to do some painting and general maintenance around the trailer park.

He was thinking maybe he could even borrow a tractor and clear a piece of land behind the trailer park. Then he would go talk to detective Williams about getting a grant from the city to put in some swing sets or a basketball court on the cleared land behind the trailer park. He just knew there must be something he could do to help those poor kids in the trailer park. Also, he spent a lot of time thinking of how he was ever going to pay supervisor Joe $11,800. Which sounded like a million dollars to Mikey.

=====================

As soon as he crosses the Arkansas line he starts looking for a truckstop so he can fuel up his truck. Then he sees a billboard for a (Pilot) truckstop about ten miles ahead. He pulls into the Pilot and fills both tanks on his Big Rig. Carmichael Trucking had given him a fuel card to use along the way. Then he pulled around back and parked his truck to catch up on his logbook. After finishing his paperwork he locks his truck and goes inside to use the restroom and get a cup of coffee. He left the truck running with the air conditioner on.

When he comes out of the truckstop, he notices a young lady standing beside his truck. As he walks over he just ignores the girl and tries to climb into his truck. But she starts talking to him, asking him if he wants a date. She says, "Hey baby, my name is Bianca. Do you like to party?" He said, "No thank you", and just kept on climbing. She is very pushy though and keeps asking if she can just get in his truck and talk for a while. He says no, but she won't give up.

She climbs up on the steps on the passenger side of his truck and starts knocking on the window. Mikey rolls down the window and says. "I'm sorry ma'am, would you please get off of my truck, I need to go". Again she says, "Come on baby I'm bored, I just want to talk. Let me in, Please".

Mikey puts the truck in gear and lurches forward as if to take off. He was hoping the girl would jump off and go away. But she didn't move, she was very persistent. Mikey had never seen anyone so persistent. He wasn't sure how to get rid of her. He set his parking brake and walked around the truck to the passenger side. Then he told her to get off of his truck or he was going to call the police. As soon as he mentioned the police. The girl jumped off and disappeared into the darkness behind the other trucks. Mikey was glad to get her off of his truck finally.

He decided before he left he should go inside and tell the manager that there is a prostitute in his parking lot asking for dates and climbing on trucks. So Mikey walks back into the truck stop and asks for the manager. He tells the manager all about the girl on his truck. Then the manager had him fill out an incident report. And Mikey heads back out to his truck.

As he is walking back to his truck. He quickly realizes there is no longer a trailer attached to the back of his truck. For a moment he just stops and looks dumbfounded, not believing his own eyes. Then he looks both ways and all around in a 360-degree circle. Hoping this is not his truck and there is another Carmichael Trucking truck in the parking lot.

But there was not and he quickly realizes his trailer had been stolen. Apparently when he got out to chase the girl away. He hadn't locked his truck doors. Then without realizing it wasn't locked up. He went inside to talk to the manager. And now someone had stolen his trailer full of Ford Motor Company car parts.

He was scared to death. Nothing like this had ever happened to Mikey. What should he do? Who should he call? Where in the heck is his trailer? What? How can this be possible? Craziness! Absolute craziness. Mikey just could not believe this was happening.

He ran back inside the Pilot and went straight up to the manager. He was just screaming, "Someone stole my trailer!, Someone stole my trailer! Please help me, Please!" Mikey was going out of his mind with hysteria. He was absolutely jumping up and down, shaking.

The manager said, "Calm down sir and I will try and help". Then he suggested they call the police. When the cops arrived fifteen minutes later Mikey was still pacing the floor. After the police officer calmed him down some. Mikey gave a complete statement and the officer quickly put out an All Points Bulletin (APB) over his radio. He announced over the radio that a 53-foot semi-trailer with the words (Carmichael Trucking) on the side of it. Had been stolen about 25 minutes ago from the Pilot truck stop parking lot. And was probably on I-40 but he didn't know which direction it was headed east or west.

Then Mikey spent about fifteen minutes filling out paperwork and filing a proper police report. He was sick to his stomach and thought he was going to puke as he went inside to dial the number for Carmichael Trucking. As he was explaining to the dispatcher at Carmichael, everything that had happened that evening. Just then one of the cops grabbed him by the arm and said, "Hang up, we found it, let's go"!

Mikey took off and followed two cop cars with lights and sirens blasting, east on I-40. They only went about 12 miles when Mikey noticed a semi-truck pulled over on the right-hand shoulder of the highway. It was surrounded by about eight cop cars. And it was lit up like a Christmas tree in the dark. The cops had the truck surrounded and already had the driver and a young lady in the back seat of one of their cars, cuffed and stuffed.

As Mikey pulled over with the two cops he was following. He could clearly read (Carmichael Trucking) on the back of the trailer. He also noticed the padlock was still on the back door, so it probably had not been opened. After he set his parking brake. The cops escorted him to the car where the driver and young girl were sitting in the back seat. One of the cops opened the door so Mikey could see inside and said, "Is she the girl you saw at the truck stop who called herself Bianca"? Mikey took a look and said, "Yes sir, that is definitely her". Bianca just smiled and tried to wave to Mikey but her hands were cuffed behind her back.

Apparently, after Mikey got Bianca off the side of his truck. She had found another guy that didn't have a trailer on his truck. And she had somehow talked him into stealing Mikey's trailer and running away with her. Or at least that's the only thing Mikey could think of.

The cops said that maybe she had been working with that guy for some time. Because they had had several trailers stolen in the state of Arkansas in the past year. But either way, they said they would soon get to the bottom of the story. Now that these two were in custody, thanks to Mikey's quick actions.

After checking the lock on the back door and walking around the trailer several times looking for any damage. The police checked Mikey's paperwork for his load and let him disconnect the trailer from the criminal's truck and reconnect it to his truck. They told Mikey he could be called on to testify in the trial against these two crooks. Then Mikey shook the hand of several of the officers and told them thanks for their quick response time. Then he took off down the highway again.

He was headed east and didn't want to go back. But he was thinking, he wished he had thanked the manager back at the Pilot for all of his help. Mikey was very relieved to finally have his trailer back and be on the road to making his delivery. He was thinking he would never leave his doors unlocked again.

At the next truckstop he could find. He stopped and called Carmichael's Trucking and explained that everything was fine and he was once again headed to West Virginia.

The rest of the trip was pretty boring except for the unbelievably beautiful scenery he saw while driving through

Tennessee. Mountains and trees and rivers and forests everywhere. Just beautiful. Mikey really felt like a lucky guy, he loved his job. As he drove farther east he wondered how many people could honestly say that they truly loved their job.

The following day Mikey made his delivery at the Ford Motor plant in Wheeling West Virginia. Then he found the Walmart warehouse and picked up the load of water bottles and headed south. He had a giant smile on his face, knowing he was going home. Man, he loved his job…He planned to stop at that Pilot truckstop on his way back through and thank the manager for all of his help in recovering the stolen trailer.

Chapter Eight
<u>D9 Cat</u>

Today Mikey has been called on to work at a local construction site. Supervisor Ted gives him the address and tells him to go see Bob at Hoopers Construction and do whatever Bob needs to be done for the day. So Mikey heads out early because he knows construction guys like to start at the crack of dawn. Especially on those hot Texas summer days. The earlier the better.

Mikey ends up driving a dump truck for the first part of the morning, hauling gravel from the rock yard to the construction site. On his third trip from the yard. His pager goes off just as he is pulling into the job site. He runs over and tells Bob he needs to leave immediately because there is (an emergency). There is a house fire and he is the fill-in firetruck driver. Anytime Mikey's pager goes off. He knows to drop everything and go to the firehouse as quickly as possible. They page him with the code (911), and he immediately knows it's a fire.

It turns out to be an apartment fire across town. When Mikey arrives on the scene the flames are already shooting out the top of the apartment building. Mikey runs inside with the other firefighters to try and clear the building from anyone that may still be inside.

It looks like actual hell inside the building. Flames everywhere and total darkness from all the smoke. Mikey has a cowbell looking thing he uses in these situations. He's running through the fire hollering, "Fire Department!. Fire Department!", and ringing his bell as loud as he can. He runs down the hallway opening every door. Then he runs upstairs yelling, "Fire Department!", as loud as he can yell.

Just then he suddenly hears someone crying out for help. He kicks in a door and finds a teenage girl holding a small child who looks to be about a year and a half old. Mikey quickly puts his face mask on the girl and grabs the baby and covers his head with his jacket. He is carrying the baby and he tells the girl to hold on tight to the tail of his jacket and follow him out. He leads them down the hallway with flames licking him on both sides.

With ceiling tiles and the walls falling apart right in front of his eyes. He soon finds the staircase and heads downstairs. He can't breathe and he can't see anything in the pitch darkness. But he is not about to give up on these two kids. He stumbles and falls several times.

He pushes a table or something out of the way with his knee. And jumps over something flaming in front of him on the floor. He yells for the girl to jump with him. He looks down two different hallways, not sure which way to go. Then he sees a crack of daylight at the end of one of the hallways and takes off in a full sprint towards it. Squeezing the baby with both hands, with the girl trailing him holding the oversized air mask with one hand and Mikey's jacket tail in her other. He dives through the doorway and lands on the sidewalk outside.

The Medics immediately ran over to assist him with the two children. With Mikey still on his butt, holding the baby. The teenage girl ran over and threw her arms around his neck. She was crying and saying, "Thank you, Thank you, Thank you". She said, "My name is Rosemary and this is my little brother Charlie. My mother wasn't home when the fire started and we didn't know what to do. So we just hid in the back room.

Then when we tried to get out, the smoke was so thick I couldn't see anything". Mikey didn't know what to say. He just hugged her back. He had been scared to death in that fire. He really wasn't sure if they were going to make it out. That was the closest he had ever come to actually being burned in a fire. He just looked up to the sky and said, "Thank you, Jesus".

After he was checked by the paramedics Mikey finished helping the other guys put out the fire. Then he helped roll up all their hoses and headed back to the firehouse. All the firefighters shook Mikey's hand and told him he had done a great job that day.

Then Mikey headed back to the construction site. When he got to the construction site Bob said, "I need you to drive that bulldozer over there for the rest of the day". He said, "I need that old building knocked down and pushed up into a pile. Then I need all these trees knocked down and pushed up into small piles so we can burn them off".

Mikey said, "Yes sir, no problem". With the funniest look on his face. He couldn't remember ever driving a D9 Caterpillar bulldozer before. This thing was absolutely huge. The (D9) is one of the largest bulldozers that Caterpillar makes. Mikey was thinking you could just about push the whole world over with this monster piece of machinery. He climbed up into the cab to check out the controls. He thought 'Humm', no steering wheel.

It just had two brake handles and a gas pedal. You just pushed the gas pedal to make it go. Then to turn you would pull the left or right brake handle according to which way you wanted to turn. If you pulled the right brake handle it would stop the right-hand side track from turning. And since the left track was still turning. The bulldozer would turn to the right. If you just wanted to go straight ahead, you didn't use either brake handle. In a few short minutes, Mikey had the gist of it and was soon pushing that old building into a big pile of rubble.

He spent the rest of the afternoon pushing down trees and clearing the land with that giant D9 Caterpillar bulldozer. It was the strongest piece of equipment he had ever operated. It could uproot the largest trees with absolute ease.

At the end of the day, Bob shook Mikey's hand and said, "Great job, son". When Mikey got home that evening he was totally exhausted. He felt like it was a good day though. He had helped save two people's lives and put out a fire. He also learned how to operate a D9 Cat bulldozer. A pretty good day he thought, for an old truck driver...

Chapter Nine
Taxi - Taxi

Today Mikey will be filling in as a taxi driver for Checkered Cab. He will spend most of the day picking up fares at the Dallas, Fort Worth airport and taking them wherever they need to go.

The first thing this morning he went to the cab company and picked up his taxi cab. They told him to just go to the airport and pick up people and take them any place they may need to go. They said just run your meter and at the end of the day bring the money back here when you turn in your cab. They said you will get your normal hourly wage plus any tips you may make throughout the day. All the money from the meter will go here to the taxi company. Mikey said he understood. And they told him to have a good day.

Upon arrival at the airport, his first fare for the day was a sweet little old lady who needed a ride to the Sheraton Hotel in downtown Dallas. Mikey helped her into the back seat, then loaded all her luggage into the trunk of the cab. He had been living in Dallas all of his life and knew his way around town very well. Soon he was pulling up to the front of the Sheraton. He unloaded the lady's luggage and left her with the bellhop. She paid her fare for the cab ride and gave Mikey a $5 tip.

She had renewed Mikey's faith in humanity. He thought she was one of the kindest people he had ever met. Just 45 minutes into the day and he was already up by five bucks. He was thinking this was going to be a great day. It had been a long time since he had driven a taxi cab. And he was starting to remember how much fun it was. And all the nice people he had met the last time he drove a cab.

So, he drove back out to the airport and waited for his next fare. Pretty soon a well-dressed gentleman in a three-piece suit asks Mikey if he could take him to the Mavericks training center. Mikey had never been a huge basketball fan but he knew right where the Mavericks training facilities were at. So he said, "Yes sir, I certainly can". It turned out, the guy in the suit was one of Mark Cuban's assistants. And he didn't have any luggage. Just a briefcase he was carrying.

When they got to the practice facility, the man paid his fare and gave Mikey a $20 tip. Then he asked Mikey if he would like to come inside and watch today's practice session. Mikey wasn't a big fan but he was thinking, 'Man, I've never been inside the Mavericks training facilities before'. He said, "Thank you, sure I'll go in and check it out". They walked in and the man said, "You can sit over there and just watch for a while if you want to". Then he said, "Thanks for the ride, there are drinks and snacks down there at the snack bar". Then he handed Mikey his business card and walked away.

Mikey sat there for about 20 minutes watching the guys run up and down the court. Then he walked over to the snack bar and got a coke. To his surprise, everything at the snack bar was completely free. They wouldn't take his money, even though he offered. As he turned to head back to his taxi cab. He finally saw a player that he recognized. There was Dirk Nowitzki, standing right behind him at the snack bar. The only Dallas Mavericks basketball player that Mikey knew by name. When he turned around and looked up. He made eye contact with Dirk, who (at 7 foot), looked to be 12 feet tall to Mikey.

Dirk reached down and shook Mikey's hand and said, "It sure is a nice day, isn't it?" Mikey didn't know what to say. He just kinda froze for a minute. Then he said, "Can I have your autograph, Mr. Nowitzki"? Dirk smiled and said. "Sure thing". Mikey reached into his pocket, but the only thing he had was the business card Mark Cuban's assistant had handed him. So he handed it and a pen to Dirk. After Dirk had signed it, he shook Mikey's hand again and said, "I'll see you at the game".

Mikey had the biggest smile on his face as he walked back to his taxi cab.

=====================

Just as Mikey jumped into the cab his pager went off, showing 911. Mikey knew he was about 20 minutes away from the firehouse. He decided to just drive the cab straight to the firehouse rather than waste time going back for his personal vehicle. He drove as fast as he could and made it to the firehouse in 18 minutes.

As he pulled up, he could see there was something weird going on. There were people everywhere, the parking lot was completely full of cars. There was a small stage set up in front, with a live band playing. There were two giant smokers in one corner with firemen handing out hotdogs and hamburgers to the crowd. There must have been 100 people out there.

Mikey couldn't find a parking space. He had to park across the street in the grocery store parking lot and walk over. He walked right up to the battalion chief and said, "Hey Chief, what's going on? Where is the fire?" The chief turned around and said, "Mikey, My Boy!". "This party is all for you, there is no fire today". Mikey was dumbfounded, he didn't know what to say.

Just then someone pulled on Mikey's arm. He turned around to see Rosemary holding little Charlie by the hand. Mikey had a big smile on his face as Rosemary reached up and gave him a big hug. She said, "Mikey this is my mother Maria, Mom this is Mikey. The guy who saved me and Charlie from the fire".

Mikey's eyes were as big as saucers as he just stared at her. He had been momentarily stunned by her beauty. She was the most beautiful creature he had ever seen. She was about three inches shorter than he was. She had long straight black hair and dark brown eyes. He thought she must be half Spanish and half white. She was wearing high heels and a dress shirt and skirt. She looked like she probably worked in an office somewhere.

He stuck out his hand and said, "Nice to meet you". Maria wasn't having a handshake though. She reached up and gave Mikey the biggest hug he had ever had. She pulled his head down close to her mouth. She said, "Thank you for saving my children". Mikey just about fell to his knees at the sound of her voice. She sounded like an angel singing in the choir of heaven. She smelled like fresh roses. His heart absolutely melted.

Just then the chief turned and pinned a brand new badge on Mikey's jacket. He said, "Son, you are now an honorary lieutenant of the Dallas County Fire department. Congratulations!" He said, "Get up on stage the mayor wants to give you a plack from the city of Dallas". Mikey hopped up on the stage. Just as the mayor said, "Let's all give a big welcome to our guest of honor Mr. Michael Van Winkle". He shook Mikey's hand and said, "Thank you, Michael, for your bravery in saving young Rosemary and Charlie's lives the other day". Then he handed Mikey a plack that read-

To Michael Van Winkle for bravery and courage in the eyes of terror. For running into the fire when everyone else is running away. For the unselfishness of risking your own life to save others. From the city of Dallas Texas with love and kindness.

Mikey took the plack and held it high in the air as the crowd cheered wildly. He then thanked the mayor and shook his hand again. Then Mikey walked over and made himself a plate with a hotdog and potato salad. As he sat and ate his lunch he could hardly keep his eyes off of Maria. Every person in the crowd came over and shook his hand or gave him a hug. Before he left, he gave his phone number to Maria and told her to stay in touch and that if she or the kids needed anything not to hesitate to call him.

After shaking everybody's hand Mikey took his new plack and walked back to his taxi cab. He decided to go back to the cab station and tell the whole story of the day's events to the cab company supervisor. The supervisor told him to take the rest of the day off. He said, "Good job Mikey you deserve it, keep up the good work, you are a good man".

With that, Mikey headed home to hang up his new plack from the city. He couldn't believe the day he had just had. He met the mayor of Dallas, and his favorite Dallas Mavericks basketball player, Dirk Nowitzki. But he couldn't stop thinking about Maria and how beautiful she was. What a day. Man, he really loved his job…

Chapter Ten
For the Children

Today Mikey will be a fill-in school bus driver for Elmwood Public Schools. He has driven school buses many times in the past twelve years. It seems like every district is always short-handed and in need of fill-in drivers. Mikey doesn't mind though, he loves working with kids. The only thing bad about driving a school bus is the hours. You have to start your route at five-thirty in the morning. Because it takes at least two hours to run your route and the kids have to be at school before 8 a.m. So you have to go to work very early in the morning.

He arrives at the bus barn at 5:30 a.m. sharp. The dispatcher hands him his route map and his bus keys. He heads out and completes his pre-trip inspection on his bus and fires it up. Quickly warming the bus up he takes off towards the northeast side of Dallas. The route takes him zig-zagging through neighborhoods. After picking up some 60 children. He has to make stops at two different grade schools before making his final drop at the North Side High School. He arrives back at the bus barn at 8:15 and parks the bus.

Mikey had already made arrangements to spend the day working at the First Baptist Church. Where he will be helping youth pastor Mark repaint and re-carpet the youth rec room today. He told Pastor Mark he would be there around 8:30.

So after parking his bus, he heads to the church. When he arrives at the church, pastor Mark is already there making coffee. Mark says, "Thanks for coming in Mikey, I really appreciate the help. We got a lot of work to do here today".

It was a beautiful day so they decided to move all the tables and furniture out onto the driveway first. Then they would put a fresh coat of paint on the walls before ripping out the old carpet. This way if they dripped any paint it wouldn't hurt the new carpet.

Mark said he had let the youth group pick out the color of the paint and carpet. The paint was a light green almost teal color and the carpet was a dark green. Mark said they were going to call it (the green room) when he and Mikey finished with it.

This room was where the church youth group did everything from arts and crafts. To practice with the youth choir and playing board games on rainy and cold Sunday afternoons. There was a piano in one corner that was the toughest obstacle for Mark and Mikey to overcome. They had to work around it all day. Moving it from one side of the room to the other. While painting, and carpeting around it.

It only took them about two hours to put a fresh coat of teal paint on the walls. Then they quickly ripped out the old shag carpet and left it lying in the driveway. The new green carpet was a more modern Berber and went down pretty easily. Again, moving the piano and working around it was the hard part. About halfway through the carpet job they took a quick lunch break and ate some sandwiched Mark's wife had made for them.

Mikey really liked youth pastor Mark. He thought of him as always being very good with the kids and a hard-working man of God. Mikey had known Mark for about three years, ever since Mark had joined their church as a youth pastor. He and Mark had completed lots of renovation projects together around the church. Mikey had great respect for youth pastor Mark. He had told Mark that anytime he needed help he could always count on Mikey.

At 2:30 they shoved the old carpet into the dumpster and tossed the last of the furniture back into the rec room. It looked beautiful and Mikey was very proud of a job well done. He and Mark just stood back and admired their work for a moment and smiled at each other. The kids would be proud of their new 'green room'. Pastor Mark shook Mikey's hand and said, "Thank you, sir, I'll see you in church".

Then Mikey took off to the bus barn to go run his three o'clock in the afternoon bus route. He just ran the route in reverse from that morning. He went to the schools and picked the children up. Then he ran backward through the neighborhoods and dropped all the kids at home. He then returned his bus to the bus barn and went inside to turn in his keys. The bus barn superintendent shook Mikey's hand and said, "Thanks Mikey, we will see you next time."

On his way home that day Mikey felt a huge sense of pride. Knowing he had helped his church and helped out that day at the shorthanded bus barn. Mikey really enjoyed his work. Every time he drove a school bus the kids were always so nice to him. They were always very thankful for the ride and would wave and smile at him as they got off the bus. He couldn't wait until the next time he would get to drive a school bus. It was one of his favorite fill-in driver jobs. He always thought that someday when he retired he might even be a full-time school bus driver. He thoroughly enjoyed the job...

Chapter Eleven
<u>Maria</u>

For the past three weeks, Mikey has thought about Maria just about every day. He thought about how sweet she had been to him and how beautiful she was. He remembered how great she smelled and how wonderful her voice sounded. But he hadn't heard anything from her and the kids. He really wanted to talk to her and maybe even get a chance to get to know her better. But he didn't know her phone number or how to get ahold of her.

He didn't even know if she was married or if she went to church or anything. Finally, he decided to go by the Apartment building where the fire had been and where he had met Rosemary and Charlie. He would ask the manager if they knew her. Or knew where she and the kids may have moved to.

Mikey drove over to the apartment complex. The damage from the fire was extensive. One side of the complex was all taped off and burnt to a crisp. It looked like there were about fifteen apartments that were completely unlivable and needed to be torn down. He just walked on by the damage and headed for the office. There was a lady behind a desk in the office.

He said, "Hi my name is Mikey. I am looking for a lady named Maria. She has a teenage daughter named Rosemary and a toddler son named Charlie. She lived here in one of the rooms that burned a few weeks ago. But I'm not exactly sure if they even still live here. Can you please help me look for her?"

The lady said, "I'm sorry sir, without the last name or an apartment number I can't give out any personal information on our residents". She said, "If you can call her and get her apartment number. I will be glad to show you where it's at". Mikey said, "Okay, I will try and call her later. Thank you very much." Then he turned and walked out the door.

As he was walking back to his car he noticed a bunch of kids playing in a fenced-in playground area. He crossed the road and walked past the fence. He didn't see anyone he recognized though. So he turned and headed back to his car. Just then he saw Rosemary walking down the sidewalk towards the playground. Her eyes caught his eyes and a big smile lit up her whole face. She ran over and gave him a big bearhug.

She said, "Hi Mikey, what are you doing here?" he said, "I was looking for you. How are you and Charlie doing?" She said, "We are doing just great. We got a new apartment on the other side of the complex. Charlie and mom are around in the swimming pool. Come on I'll show you". She grabbed his hand and drug him around the side of the building.

As soon as they entered the swimming pool area fence, Mikey saw Maria laying out on a towel in her swimsuit getting a tan. She had on shades and looked to be about half asleep on the towel. Mikey noticed Charlie splashing around in the kiddie pool. Rosemary drug Mikey right up to her mom and yelled, "Hey mom! Mikey is here! Wake up." Maria looked completely embarrassed and turned about three shades of red. She grabbed the towel and covered herself up.

She stood up and wrapped the towel around her waist. Then she looked at Mikey and said, "Hi, what are you doing here"? Mikey said, "I came to check on you guys, I haven't heard from you and I was wondering how things were going". Maria said, "We are doing good, we got a new apartment after the fire. We have been slowly collecting new furniture and things". Mikey said, "Well that is just great." Can I do anything to help"? She said, "Well since you're here, a neighbor gave us a couch and I could use some help moving it into our apartment. If you don't mind"?

Mikey said, "Yes ma'am, anything I can do to help, put me to work". They left the kids at the pool and Mikey followed her to their apartment. She invited him in and asked if he wanted something to drink. He said, "Maybe later, thank you". She went into the back room and changed. Then they went to the neighbor's place and got the couch. They had a little trouble getting it to fit through the front door. But once they cleared the door it looked really good setting in their front room. It actually matched the carpet rather well.

They sat down on the new sofa and just talked and talked and talked. They seemed like old friends who had known each other for years. Mikey found out that her husband had left two years ago after he found out she was pregnant with little Charlie. Maria said he didn't want the responsibility of having more kids and he left her shortly after she told him she was pregnant. She hadn't seen or heard from him since. He didn't contact her or the kids and he had never sent any money in the two years since he left.

Mikey felt bad for the kids, having to grow up without their dad. And little Charlie had never even met his dad. But he was kinda glad to hear she wasn't married. He couldn't take his eyes off of her. He thought she was (absolutely) stunning. He couldn't believe she was single.

Maria asked Mikey if he would stay for supper. She was cooking an enchilada casserole in the oven. Mikey had been smelling it ever since they walked into the apartment. It smelled divine and he accepted her invitation to stay. Mikey walked back to the pool area and rounded up the kids while Maria set the table.

When they walked in Rosemary said, "Cool beans, we got a new sofa". They had a wonderful dinner. The enchiladas were absolutely to die for. After dinner, Mikey read a book to Charlie while the girls cleaned up the kitchen. Afterword Maria came in and sat next to Mikey on the couch. She said, "You sure are good with kids. Do you have children?" Mikey said, "No, I have never been married. However, I almost married my high school sweetheart. But in the end, it didn't work out. Then I just never found the right girl".

He said, "I do love children though. I fill in from time to time as a school bus driver, the children are great. And I help out with the youth group at my church. I also drive the church bus". He said, "I always wanted to have kids. By the way, do you guys go to church"? Maria said, "Yes I take the kids to church just about every Sunday. We attend the non-denominational church just around the corner". He said, "Well that's just great".

They all moved to the kitchen and played a game of (boggle) until it was getting late and Mikey thought he should be going. He gave the kids a big hug and told them goodnight. Then he thanked Maria for dinner and everything. As he hugged her goodbye she reached up and kissed Mikey on the cheek, and told him he was a really nice man.

He could barely walk back to his car, his knees were so wobbly he almost tripped over his own feet several times. He was in such a daze, he wasn't even completely sure he could drive himself home....

Chapter Twelve
Bull Wagon

Today Mikey will be filling in at the stockyards. Hauling cows from the stock pens on the south side of town across the scales at the stockyards on the north side of town. This is going to be a new experience for Mikey. He has never hauled cattle before.

First thing this morning he picks up his truck and trailer at Express Bulls on the southwest side of Dallas. The supervisor is a man named Frank Barnes. Frank follows Mikey out to the bullpens to show him how to load the cattle into the truck and also to tell him which pens he wants to be emptied today.

Mikey hadn't realized it yet, but this is a one-man operation. He will have to load the cows into his trailer and take them across the scale at the stockyards on the north side of Dallas. Mikey will be responsible for getting the right cows to the market and for keeping a tally of how much each load weighs.

Mikey soon finds out, the hard part of this job is getting the cattle into the truck and also getting the right ones on each trip. Frank tells Mikey he needs the three most western side pens emptied today. Then Frank stays and helps Mikey get his first load of cattle loaded up for the day. Mikey learns you can put a lot of cows into your trailer on each load. Because the trailer has two levels, like a double-decker bus. You can put about 22 cows on each deck. So altogether he can carry 44 cows to the market on each trip. The tricky part is getting them to climb up into the truck.

Frank shows Mikey the easy way to get the cows onto the truck. First, you back your truck up to the loading chute. Then you take an electrical shock prod and prod the first cow up the chute. Then the other cows will pretty much follow the first one. You just close the gate after you count 22. Then you drop the ramp going up to the top deck of your trailer and do the whole thing all over again until you have 22 more cows on the bottom deck. Then you secure the back door and you're ready to go to the market.

Mikey thinks that it wasn't too bad. As long as the cows cooperate, he should have a good day. And hopefully, he will get all of Franks cows to the market safely. Frank said he had about 260 head of cattle he needed to get to the stockyards today.

So before he takes off Mikey does the math. If he can haul 44 cows at a time and he needs to get 260 to the market today. He will have to make six trips back and forth. No problem, it's about a 25-minute drive each way from the cattle pens to the stockyards. If he can load and unload the cows pretty quickly he should be able to get all the cows to market in an eight or ten-hour day.

He takes off up the highway with that first load and quickly realizes this is a little different than any other freight he has ever hauled. He had never thought about it, but with all those cows moving around back there. The truck is constantly swaying from side to side. The driver has to pay close attention and correct, or oversteer every time the truck sways to one side. Mikey has never hauled (live) animals before. This is going to be an experience for sure.

After about 30 minutes Mikey is setting on the scale at the stockyards, waiting to get his (weighed in) ticket. He then pulled around to the chute and unloaded his cattle. After weighing out he heads back to the Express Bullpens. He checks his (in) and (out) tickets and learns that those 44 cows weighed just over 52,000 pounds. Which he figured up to almost 1200 pounds a cow. Mikey thought (wow), that's a lot of hamburgers.

On his way back to the pens he thought a lot about Maria and the kids. He just remembered he hadn't asked Maria what she did for a living. He also wondered what school Rosemary went to. For the next couple of hours, he just ran back and forth between the bullpens and the stockyard scale. It was a fairly straight forward job, just time-consuming.

At lunchtime, he stopped by O'Malley's Towing Service and gave supervisor Joe another payment on the damaged truck. He again told Joe how sorry he was for the damages. Joe said, "Oh, son, don't worry too much. These things usually have a way of working out. I'm sure some of the stuff will be recovered by the police. If not the insurance company will reimburse me for most of it". Mikey said, "Yeah, but I still feel really bad, and I will pay you back every penny".

Just as Mikey was walking out the door his pager went off with a number he didn't recognize. He went back inside and asked Joe if he could use the phone. Joe said, "Sure thing Mike". He dialed the number and to his surprise, it was Maria who picked up the phone. She asked if he would like to meet her for lunch. He explained that he would love to, but he was busy hauling these cows all day.

She said, "Well why don't you come for dinner then"? Mikey said, "I would absolutely love that, you are an awesome cook, thank you. But it will have to be late because I am not going to get these cows all in until probably around seven o'clock". She said, "Fine, we will see you at eight then". He smiled and hung up the phone. He said, "Thanks Joe", and then walked outside.

The rest of the day went smooth as silk. With Mikey thinking about Maria and wondering what was for dinner. He got all of the cattle to the market on time and safely. Then he parked his truck back at the Express Bull's main office and headed home for a quick shower and change of clothes.

Along the way, he stopped for a bottle of wine and got to Maria's place at 8 o'clock sharp. The kids came running, with hugs all around, they were very happy to see him. Maria said, "Thanks for the wine". Then she asked him about his day and how he liked the cattle business. He said it wasn't a bad job. But the cows really (stink) and can be cantankerous sometimes when you are trying to get them onto the truck. Everybody got a good laugh out of that.

Mikey sat on the sofa with the kids while Maria finished preparing dinner. Rosemary asked Mikey if he would like to see her room. He said sure, and the next thing he knew she was dragging him and Charlie down the hallway. After looking at her new bed and all of her stuffed animals. Mikey noticed a poster on the backside of the door of the Dallas Mavericks basketball team. He asked Rosemary if she liked the

Dallas Mavericks. She said, "I'm their biggest fan, I am going to marry Dirk Nowitzki when I grow up". He just smiled and said, "I bet you are".

At the dinner table Mikey looked at Maria and said, "I hear Rosemary is a big fan of the Mavericks basketball team". Maria said, "Yes, she watches every game on TV and has been trying to get me to take her to a game for years. She is their biggest fan. She thinks she is in love with some guy named Lavenski or something".

Rosemary said, "Nowitzki mom! Dirk Nowitzki." Mikey laughed and reached into his pocket to pull out his wallet. He handed Rosemary a business card and smiled. She began reading it out loud. It said, "Mr. Samuel Farmington, assistant for team directors". With a puzzled look on her face, she looked at Mikey and said, "What the heck is a Samuel Farmington"?

Mikey said, "Turn it over". She flipped it over and again read out loud. It said, "Keep on smiling" - Dirk Nowitzki # 41. She just about fell out of her chair. She said, "Is this his actual autograph"? Mikey said, "Yeah the guy on the front of that card was a passenger in my taxi cab last week. He let me go inside the practice facility and watch the team practice. I saw Dirk at the snack bar and asked him for his autograph. He was a really nice guy. He was always smiling." Rosemary ran to her room screaming and kissing and hugging the business card.

Mikey then asked Maria where she worked. She said she worked for a local insurance company and she processed claims all day. She said basically she just sat behind a computer and filled out paperwork all day. But she enjoyed her work and had been working there for almost ten years. She said it provided her and the kids a pretty good life. She said they may not have everything they wanted, but they had everything they needed. Mikey said, "Well, that's all you can ask the good lord for". Maria smiled at him.

After another wonderful dinner of lemon peppered grilled chicken and steamed vegetables. They all took a walk around the park behind the apartment complex. When they got back it was bedtime for the kids. Mikey gave them each a big hug and told them goodnight. Rosemary kissed him on the cheek and thanked him again for the Nowitzki autograph.

He and Maria sat on the sofa and had a glass of wine. Mikey wasn't much of an alcohol drinker. However, he did enjoy a cold glass of Sangria from time to time. Especially with the right company. They again just talked and talked and talked about everything. It was as if they had been friends forever. Before Mikey knew it, it was getting late and he thought he should go and let Maria get some rest.

He hugged her goodbye at the door and thanked her again for another great evening. He said he truly enjoyed spending time with her and the kids. Then they embraced and had their first (real) kiss. When Mikey pulled away his face was blushing and he could feel his heart just melting. The smile on Maria's face said it all. He said, "Goodnight pretty lady". As he turned to leave, she said, "That was a really sweet thing you did for Rose"…

Chapter Thirteen
<u>Mardi Gras</u>

Today Mikey is filling in at Snodgrass Charters. Where he will be driving a tour busload of senior citizens from Dallas Texas to New Orleans Louisiana. For an overnight stay at the Mardi Gras celebration. Mikey has never been to Mardi Gras and is very much looking forward to this trip.

It is about 500 miles from Dallas Texas to New Orleans Louisiana. It will take Mikey about ten hours to drive the bus down there, counting stopping in the middle for a quick meal and fuel. So the plan is to leave at 6 a.m. from the Snodgrass Charters parking lot.

All the people going on this trip are from two local retirement communities there in Dallas. There will be 38 passengers on the bus. Mikey actually knows a couple from his church, Mr. Barnes and his wife Ella. He has known them for many years and thinks the world of them. They also think he is a very nice young man.

Luckily everyone shows up on time and Mikey gets them and all their luggage loaded up and ready to go. He has already completed his pre-trip inspections and the bus is warmed up and ready to go. He has the whole trip planned out. He will take I-20 east to Shreveport. Then go south on I-49 through Louisiana. Then take I-10 east into New Orleans.

They planned to take a small detour and drive through the town of Natchitoches. Natchitoches is one of the original Louisiana colonies and has some very old and beautiful houses and plantations around it. Everyone is looking forward to the drive through Natchitoches. Plus they should get there right around lunch break time.

The first leg of their journey is still in the dark, so Mikey has to really concentrate on his driving. He turned the radio on but kept the volume pretty low. He notices that most of his passengers are sleeping anyway. Pretty soon he is watching the sun come up right in front of him. The day is partly cloudy and the temperature is just right. Mikey enjoys the drive across Texas and into Louisiana.

A couple of hours later he pulls into Natchitoches. He announces over his intercom to make sure everyone is awake. He says, "Your attention please Natchitoches, Natchitoches". He then takes the long way through Natchitoches. Driving by some beautiful old homesteads and bed & breakfast. Old cathedral-style churches and old farmhouses. Everyone took a lot of pictures along the way.

They stopped for a few minutes at a 300-year-old plantation. They bought homemade jams and loaves of bread and enjoyed the view of the farmlands. There was even a small petting zoo. Back on the highway, they find a truck stop to get fuel and some sandwiches. Mikey gets a cup of coffee and a power bar for the road. After a quick fuel stop, they are back on schedule.

They make it to New Orleans at about 4:30 in the afternoon. It looks to Mikey like there are twice as many people and traffic in New Orleans than there is in Dallas. He had never seen such a crazy site. The people are all dressed in funny looking costumes and masks. Even their cars are decorated in what looks like parade wear. The whole city is decorated with funny signs and lights and beads. It reminds him of Christmas decorations.

It takes Mikey almost an hour to get everyone unloaded in front of the hotel and find a parking place for the bus. He secures the bus and grabs his overnight bag to go find his room. As soon as he enters the hotel he realizes he is in a different world. There are all kinds of weird carnival looking masks hanging all around the lobby and all kinds of lights and decorations. Everybody in the lobby is either wearing a mask or a funny-looking hat. Everything from funny clown hats to jester looking hats with balls on the ends.

Mikey just walked around the lobby for a minute taking it all in. Then he walks up to the counter to ask for his room keys and check in. A guy pops up from behind the counter wearing what looks like a clown suit with a (Where's Waldo) looking shirt and a long Santa Claus beard. He says, "*You Rang*? I'll be your ticket master today, do you need a single or a double"? Mikey says, "Single please, I have a reservation". The guy said, "*Your-Name-Please*". In a voice that sounded like (Lurch) from the Addams Family. Mikey answered him with, "Michael Van Winkle".

The guy said, "Van Winkle, what is that German"? Mikey said, "I'm not sure, it may be Dutch". Then he grabbed his keys and left. This guy was a little bit south of weird. Mikey found his room and took a quick shower.

Then he called Maria before it got too late. He told her he missed her and he would be back late tomorrow night. He said he wasn't planning on leaving the room much, except to get something to eat. He said, "There are some very strange characters running around down here in Louisiana. I'm not sure about this Mardi Gras thing".

He asked her how the kids were doing. She said they were fine, Rosemary had been showing off her (Dirk Nowitzki) autograph to everyone they knew. Charlie was playing with one of the neighbor kids. He told her he was going to get something for dinner, then get some rest before the drive back tomorrow. He told her goodnight and said he would see her soon. He told her to give the kids hugs for him and she said she would.

Then he went downstairs to look for some food. He bumped into a bellhop at the bottom of the stairs that looked to be one of the Village People with a Phantom of the Opera mask on. He said, "Excuse me". Then he heard live music coming from the street in front of the hotel. He stepped out onto the sidewalk to see a parade going past.

There was a marching band with funny costumes. Followed by a float being pulled by 12 guys with ropes tied around their waist, all dressed as the flying monkeys from the (Wizard of Oz). The float was being pushed by three guys. One dressed as a Lion, one dressed as a Tin Man, and one dressed as a Scarecrow. There was a man on the float dressed as (The Wicked Witch). He was singing what sounded to Mikey like French opera music. Mikey said out loud, "Man, we are definitely not in Kansas anymore".

Just then someone tapped Mikey on the shoulder. He turned around to see Mr. and Mrs. Barnes from his church. Ella said,

"We are all going to the restaurant across the street if you would like to join us for dinner". Mikey said, "Yes, thank you, I sure will, I'm starving. Just lead the way." They crossed the street and ate real creole food for dinner. Which Mikey had also never experienced before. He didn't eat any mudbugs, (they looked scary), but he got his fill of catfish and rice.

Then he got up and thanked everyone for the dinner. He told them to have fun tonight but he needed to get some rest for the drive back in the morning. He told them the bus would be ready to leave after breakfast at about 9:30. Then he said goodnight and went to his room.

For two hours he tried to go to sleep. But all the noise outside kept him awake. He walked over to the balcony two or three times and looked out at the endless parade walking down the street. On the third trip as he walked back to his bed. He noticed a pair of headphones hanging from the headboard. He slipped them over his head and heard the most soothing sounds he had ever heard. It was a babbling brook with birds chirping in the background. He figured the hotel hung those there so people could get some sleep.

With the headphones on, he slept like a baby. Before he knew it, the sunshine coming through the window woke him up. He had a quick shower and got dressed. He took his overnight bag downstairs with him so he wouldn't have to go back. He handed Lurch his room keys and went to the cafe for breakfast and coffee.

There were already several people from his group in the cafe eating breakfast. He told them after he ate he would go warm up the bus and pull it around to the east side of the hotel. He said he would park by the curb so they could all load up their luggage.

Mikey completed his pre-trip inspection on the bus and pulled around to the east side of the building. He couldn't pull in front of the hotel because the parade had been going all night and was now going into the day. A bellhop dressed as a gargoyle with a werewolf mask met Mikey at the curb with all the luggage. They quickly loaded it into the undercarriage bins on the bus. He said, "Thank you for the help Mr. Werewolf".

Then he did a headcount and loaded 38 passengers onto the bus.

After fighting bumper to bumper traffic for almost an hour. They were finally back on the highway and headed toward Dallas. Mikey enjoyed the drive home. Slow and steady like his dad had taught him to drive as a teenager. Mikey never got in a hurry, especially when he was carrying passengers. He considered them to be the most precious cargo he could haul. He was glad to be out of the traffic in New Orleans and headed north. He had fun on this trip but was more than ready to go home. Plus he missed Maria and the kids.

On the ride home, he pondered how much he loved his job. He wondered how many people could say they truly loved what they were doing for a living. He couldn't believe that Ted at (Part-Time Drivers), actually paid him to go out and drive around and have fun all day. What a job, Mikey really loved his job. He thought a guy couldn't have more fun and get paid for it unless he was a circus clown. He also pondered about having a wife and children.

He wondered what Maria thought about getting remarried.

They pulled back into the Snodgrass Charters parking lot about 7:30 that evening. Everyone at Snodgrass had already gone home for the day. So Mikey spent about an hour unloading everyone's luggage and helping them get it into their cars. They all shook his hand and told him thanks for a job well done. He locked the bus up and put the keys in the dropbox by the front office. Then he headed home for the day.

With a feeling of content, for another great day. He sat down and dialed Maria's number. He said, "Hey beautiful, I miss you". She said, "I was just about to call and see if you made it home yet. How was your trip?" He said, "There are some strange characters at Mardi Gras. We will have to go someday." They talked for about an hour about his trip and just about life in general. He asked her if she had ever thought about getting remarried. She said she would love to have a father figure around for the kids. And she thought Mikey was an awesome man. He said, "You're pretty sweet too girly".

He told her he didn't know if he was ready to get married. But all he knew was that he really, really missed her and the kids when he was away from them. And he had always wanted a family. He said, "I love you sweetie, goodnight". And with that, he was out like a light…

Chapter Fourteen
<u>Aquarium</u>

The following day was Saturday. The phone woke Mikey up at seven a.m. A voice said, "Good morning handsome man". He smiled at the sweet sound of her voice. And said, "Good morning yourself beautiful". Maria said, "The kids and I are going to the Aquarium today and wondered if you would like to join us"? Mikey jumped out of bed and said, "Yes, ma'am. What time are you going?" She said, "They open at nine". He said, "Okay, let me take a shower and get dressed. Do you want me to pick you guys up?" She replied, "Yes Sir, Please".

When he arrived at Maria's place he gave the kids big hugs. Even though it had only been about a week since he had seen then, it seemed like a year to Mikey. He kissed and hugged Maria and told her that he had really missed them.

They took the kids to McDonald's for breakfast. It was Rosemary and Charlie's favorite place to eat. They arrived at the Dallas Aquarium just after 9 a.m. Mikey asked Maria if she had ever been to the aquarium before. She said she and the kids had been there many times. She said the first time she ever went was about six years ago on a field trip with Rosemary's class. Since then she had brought the kids back 5 or 6 times. That they always had a good time and just loved the aquarium. She said they loved the shark tanks the best.

Maria then asked Mikey if he had ever been to the aquarium. He said it was his mother's favorite place to take him when he was a child. He said his mom just loved the manta rays. That she would sit and watch them for hours. She loved their grace and the way they seemed to be flying through the water like a bird soaring through the sky. As he smiled talking about his mother, Marie could see the fondness of the memories in his face.

Maria said, "You have never told me about your parents. Do they live here in Dallas"? He said, "Let's talk about that later. How about we go see some fish"? Rosemary and Charlie were already running ahead of them, heading for the tanks of octopus. They spent the next few minutes feeding the octopus. Then made a mad dash for the shark tanks. There was a giant glass tunnel where you could walk under the shark tank and see the sharks from all angles. Charlie absolutely loved them, he went bananas in the tunnel trying to catch a shark.

After two hours of walking through the aquarium. Mikey and Maria sat down in front of the manta ray tank. Mikey said this was my mother's favorite place in the whole wide world. With tears in his eyes, he said, " When I was 19 years old my parents died in a car wreck. It was one winter night during a terrible blizzard. They were going to church for a Christmas program by our youth group. I was already at the church because we had a final practice and I was in the youth choir".

He said, "Their car slid off the interstate and they were both pronounced dead at the scene. I rushed to the hospital and tried to help, but there was nothing anybody could do". He said, "I was about to enter college on a scholarship, but I never went. I sat at home and cried for a month".

He told Maria how he had never talked to anyone about his parent's death. He said his mother was a school teacher and had been his inspiration growing up. He was an only child and had been very close to his parents. His father had taught him everything from how to tie his shoes, to how to drive a car. He got his love of driving from his father. But his mother was the one who led him through life and made him the person he turned out to be.

She had driven him to school every day of his life. Since she was a teacher, she was going anyway. Even after Mikey got his driver's license. He still rode with his mother every morning to school, his whole life. They would talk about schoolwork or any other problems Mikey had. His mom was always a good listener, and she usually had the answer to whatever problems he may be dealing with. When his parents died, he couldn't force himself to go to college. Knowing that his mom wouldn't be there to help him along the way.

He told Maria that he still lived in the only house he had ever lived in. It was his parent's house that he had grown up in. He had remodeled it several times over the years and even turned his parent's old room into a garage. But was never able to bring himself to sell it or move away. He remembered how much his parents had loved that house.

He said about a year after his parent's car wreck he joined the Army. He spent four years in the Army. Where he realized his love for driving trucks. He said he went through the Army's driver training program and got his CDL, Commercial Drivers License, while he was in the middle east. He said he spent two years in the middle east and never once discharged his weapon. He said he spent all of his time driving delivery trucks and personnel carriers. Delivering people and supplies from one base to another. Driving wherever he was needed.

When he got out of the military, he had enough money in the G.I. Bill program that he could have gone to college for free. But again, he couldn't talk himself into going back to school without his parents being here. So he never went back to school.

He told Maria he had been working for Ted at Part-Time Driver for the past twelve years. Before that, he had driven an 18-wheeler across the country for a couple of years. He said the Army, the 18-wheeler, and working for Ted were the only three jobs he had ever had.

Then he looked up and said, "When I was young, my mother brought me to this aquarium probably 4 or 5 times a year. She just loved the Manta Rays, this was her favorite spot."

Maria put her arms around him and said, "I'm so sorry baby, I love you so much. You are the sweetest, most honest man I have ever met. I hope we stay together forever and ever". Mikey wiped his tears and kissed her. He said, "I love you too girly".

They rounded up the kids and headed to Mikey's house. Where he and Maria cooked dinner that evening together. After dinner, they played board games and talked about Mikey getting a dog. Maria and the children spent the night at Mikey's house that night. The next morning they all went to Maria's house to change clothes. Then they all went to The First Baptist Church together. Mikey introduced Maria and the children to everybody he knew at his church.

Charlie and Rosemary had a blast in Sunday school. Rosemary said they did arts and crafts in her class and Charlie said he made 100 new friends. Maria was all smiles as they shook hands with everyone on their way out of the church. Mikey took them next door and showed them the (green room) he and pastor Mark had recently remodeled. It was full of teenagers who seemed to really be enjoying it.

Mikey held Maria's hand as they walked to the car, with the kiddos skipping in time behind them….

Chapter Fifteen
<u>Seeing Stars</u>

Mikey will be filling in as the Zamboni driver at tonight's hockey game between the Dallas Stars and the New Jersey Devils. Mikey has driven a Zamboni many times in the past and he loves it. He has to go out before the game and (shave), or resurface the ice, to get it ready for the game. Then he has to re-smooth it at every time out or break the teams may take during the game. This way the ice stays as smooth as possible and doesn't get all rutted up by the skaters.

The Zamboni driver has a pretty easy job and he gets a lot of perks from the team and the arena owners. Like he gets all the free food and drinks he wants from the snack bar. He also gets free tickets, for him and his family, to any games he may be working at. Mikey loves driving the Zamboni. He thinks it's a cool job.

Tonight he has asked Maria and the kids to join him at the Dallas Stars arena to watch the game. The game starts at seven, but Mikey has to be there an hour early to get the ice ready. He picks up Maria and the kids and heads to the arena at about 5:30.

Mikey is a little concerned about tonight's game because the opposing team from New Jersey has a much better record than his Dallas Stars this year. Plus they have one of the best goaltenders in the league. He is just about impossible to score on. A guy by the name of Martin Brodeur, who is one of the very best at his craft. He has stopped more shots than Bill Doolin in Oklahoma territory in 1896. He slapped so many shots out of the net, that guys are scared to shoot against him. So Mikey is a little worried about Dallas's chances tonight.

The manager for the Dallas Stars is a man named Bartholomew Jackson, that Mikey went to high school with. Jackson was the starting quarterback for the Western Heights Blue Jays in the late 1980s. Mikey was a starting defensive back on that same team. They had been very close friends in high school and even shared a locker at one time.

Bart, as Mikey called him. Was from a wealthy oil family. His father owned an oil and gas company back in the '70s and '80s. That he later sold and it became OTX Energy. By the '90s the Jackson family were millionaires. After high school, Bart got a full-ride scholarship and played football for the Texas A&M Aggies. After college he was a very successful businessman in the Dallas, Ft. Worth area, owning several car dealerships.

Mikey always figured he got the management job with the Dallas Stars because his father was part owner of the team. He and Bart had gone their separate ways after Bart went off to A&M and Mikey joined the Army. They had only spoken a few times since. The few times that Mikey had run the Zamboni at the ice arena.

But tonight Mikey planned on cornering Bart. And asking him if Rosemary and Charlie could stay after the game and skate around with the players and maybe even get a few autographs.

By halftime, it wasn't looking very good. Dallas was down two to nothing. Mikey resurfaced the ice during the halftime break. He could see Maria, Rosemary, and Charlie all waving at him from their seats.

He waved back and quickly made his rounds with the Zamboni. Then as the team came back out onto the court he stopped Bart and said hi. Then he asked if he and the kids could stay after the game and do a little skating. Bart said, "Sure Mike, it's nice to see you, buddy. Stay as long as you want and have fun with the kids".

Dallas lost the game three to one. But everyone had a blast cheering on the team. After the game, Mikey ran through the crowded arena and found Maria. He told Rosemary and Charlie to follow him. He said, "I have a surprise for you guys". He took them downstairs and had them fitted for ice skates. Then he and Maria also put on a pair. They all went out onto the ice together. Charlie kept falling and every one slipped and slid everywhere. None of them were the greatest skaters in the world. But they had an absolute ball on the ice.

As they skated around they got to meet several of the players doing their warm down. The kids were so excited they could have burst. The players were all so nice. They seemed to really enjoy skating around with the children. Mikey and Maria had the time of their lives. They skated around holding hands for almost an hour. Every time one of them fell, they would try to catch each other and both fall down. They laughed and played and skated like they were children themselves.

By the end, they were all exhausted and ready to go home. Mikey went and put up the Zamboni and all of his equipment. Then he took them all back to Maria's house and helped her tuck in the children. Mikey and Maria then sat down and talked the night away. This time they talked about the future. He told Maria he was thinking about taking a full-time job driving a trolley for the city of Dallas. He said the mayor had called and offered him the job personally.

He told her if he took the job it would mean a pay raise and full benefits from the city. Plus he would be putting in time and money towards retirement. Which he had never done before. He said lately he had been seriously thinking about settling down and having a family. Which would mean having a steady job and not being gone all the time. Then he said, if the right woman would marry him, he would even consider selling his house and buying a bigger one. She smiled.

After rambling for twenty minutes he felt a little embarrassed and tried to change the subject. He said, "I never asked you about your parents". Maria said, "I was born in San Juan and I lived in Puerto Rico until I was three years old. My father drowned in a boating accident when I was only two years old. My mother then brought me and my sister to live with our aunt in Florida, when I was three years old".

She said, "My mother passed away when I was eleven from a rare form of leukemia. Then my aunt sent me and my sister to Texas to live with our Grandmother. I have lived within 40 miles of here ever since." He said, "What about your Grandmother? Is she still alive?" She said, "Yes, she lives in a nursing home in Waco. The last few times I visited her, she didn't even know my name. She has Alzheimer's or something. She is 82 years old". She said, "My sister now lives in Albuquerque with her husband and two kids. She is a dental assistant, we only see each other every few years".

Mikey said, "I'm sorry sweetie, your story sounds a lot like mine". They both smiled at each other. Every time they had stayed up half the night talking, Mikey fell in love with her all over again. He spent the night again that night and did not want to go back home again. He knew he wanted to spend the rest of his life with Maria. He loved her more than he had ever loved anyone in his whole life.

He couldn't believe he could find such a beautiful and perfect woman. He thanked God every day for bringing Maria and her kids into his life. He had decided to give his two-week notice to Ted at (Part-Time Drivers). Then he would take the job with the city and drive a trolley for a living. Mikey's life couldn't be any better, he was so happy...

Chapter Sixteen
<u>The Long Road Home</u>

Today Mikey is back at Carmichael's trucking. Where he will be filling in once again as a long-haul truck driver. He will be driving an 18-wheeler from the Dollar General Store warehouse in Dallas Texas to Bakersfield California. He will be hauling pretty much everything they sell in a Dollar General Store. He will be delivering his load to a brand new store that has just opened up in Bakersfield. Then he will go to the Michelin Tire plant in Bakersfield and get a load of car tires and bring them back to Dallas.

This trip is almost 1500 miles each way and he will have to go across Texas, New Mexico, Arizona and half of California. This will be an epic trip for Mikey, one of the longest he has ever made. He only took the job because he knew in a few weeks his trucking career would be over. He wanted one last road trip before saying goodbye.

Early this morning before the rooster even started crowing. Mikey pulls up to

Carmichael Trucking and starts his pre-trip inspection. He is careful to check everything twice. He knows this is a very long hard trip and he doesn't want to have any mechanical problems with the truck. Mr. Carmichael told Mikey the night before that the truck was loaded and ready to go. The keys were under the floor mat and the load documentation was under the sun visor.

Mikey first checks the lock on the back door, to make sure no one has tampered with it overnight. Then he checks his tires and lights. Then he checks that all the brakes are working properly. Once he is ready to go, he stops and says a small prayer. He asks God to keep him safe and allow him to relax and enjoy his final journey in a Big Rig. He is thinking about Maria as he pulls out onto the open road.

It's a fairly straight shot from Dallas to Bakersfield. If you just go west you can hardly miss it. The main problem is that it's a long trip and you have to cross the Mojave desert. The heat of the desert is very hard on a big heavy truck. Mikey will take several breaks along the way. He will make sure his truck has plenty of water and he has plenty of water. It will take Mikey about six days to complete his mission. He will just drive all day, then sleep in the bunk on his truck at night. He will shower every other day at truck stops when he stops to get fuel.

The first leg of his journey takes him northwest across Texas where he picks up I-40 in Amarillo. For the next two and a half days, he will follow I-40 west into Bakersfield California. It's a straight shot from Amarillo to Bakersfield. It is a hot sunny day in Texas. He can only imagine how hot it's going to get driving through Arizona and California.

The truck seems to be running well. It is pulling the load along very well. With a heavy load like this Mikey has to be on his toes. It takes a long time for him to get the truck up to speed. But Mikey also knows it takes a lot of room to stop the truck. So he is constantly watching his following distance between cars. As he drives he remembers what his dad taught him when he was a teenager. Slow and steady always wins the race. Slow and steady…

By the second day, Mikey is ready to find a nice truckstop and take a shower and also fill his fuel tanks. He pulls into a Flying J truck stop in Winslow Arizona, just outside Flagstaff. He fills his fuel tanks and parks his truck around behind the truck stop. After making sure to lock his doors. He goes inside the truckstop and has dinner with a fellow truck driver he just met from Arkansas named Robert.

At dinner all Robert talks about is being on the road all the time away from his family, and how much he misses his wife and kids. Robert says he hasn't been home in three weeks. He even missed his son's birthday last month. He says he wasn't home for Christmas last year either. Robert says he has been out on the road for almost nine years and his kids have grown up without him around.

Robert says he used to go to family get-togethers and outings with his friends. He used to go out on Friday nights with his wife. He said life is just passing him by. His wife and he are both getting old. His kids are just about grown. And he has missed everything with them.

This all makes Mikey sad. He was already missing Maria and the kids something terrible. After talking with Robert he realizes why he has to give up truck driving and take that city job. He can't stand to be away from Maria and the kids. It's going to tear his heart out to be gone for another four days.

As soon as he finishes his dinner he goes and calls Maria. He tells her how much she means to him and how much he loves her. He says he can't wait to get back to Dallas and see her beautiful smile. He says he realizes that she completes him and that she is the woman he has been looking for his entire life. He says, "I love you so much girly. You have my heart and everything that goes with it".

He told her that he gave his two-week notice to Ted at Part-Time Driver before he left Dallas. He said, "This is my last road trip baby. I'm coming home for good. I will never go anywhere without you and the kids again, as long as I live. I love you, Maria." She told him how much she loved him too and they said goodnight.

Then he showered and got a good night's sleep in his truck. He rolled out before sunup the next morning and arrived in Bakersfield just before dark the next day. He drove right to the Dollar General store as if he had been there 100 times. He docked his truck behind the store and it only took about an hour and a half for two forklift operators to get his trailer unloaded.

As soon as he was emptied, he asked the guy who signed his paperwork where he could find the Michelin Tire Factory. It was just across town and easy to get to. At Michelin, he didn't have to wait to get reloaded. He just had to drop his trailer and hook onto an already loaded trailer and go. He thought, 'Man these Michelin guys are on the ball. Trailers are already loaded and waiting, how nice is that'. Before you knew it, he was headed back east.

The return trip to Dallas was long and hot. That old Peterbilt did a great job though. Mikey made very good time. Just short of six days and he was back home. Back home for good. He had a lot of time to think out on the road. He reminisced about his life and about his parents. He thought about how great his life would be with Maria and the kids being together as a family. He thanked God for his life and all of his many blessings.

He had a rough time after his parents died. But looking back now he realized he had always been a good man. He had always tried to do the right thing and treat people right. He had always tried to live his life right and be an honest man. He was sure he now deserves to be happy and have a family again. He couldn't wait to get home to Maria. He would love her and cherish her and take care of her for the rest of his life. He thanked God. He really felt like a blessed man.

When he got back to Maria's house, his heart just fell into his stomach. As he embraced her, he knew he was (home) with his family. Where he belonged, and where he would now be able to stay forever...

Chapter Seventeen
<u>Redemption</u>

After Mikey returned from his trip to California he spent the entire weekend with Maria and her kids. Charlie had his second birthday and after the party, Mikey took them all fishing to celebrate. Charlie had never been fishing before. All he caught was a small perch, but he had a smile the size of Texas as he reeled it in.

Today is Monday, and his final week working for Ted at Part-Time Drivers. Today Mikey will be a fill-in transit bus driver on the campus of the University of North Texas at Dallas.

He will be driving a transit bus around the campus hauling students and faculty from building to building. He has a specific route with stops clearly marked where people can ride the bus to different classes or to the parking lot where they may be parked. Or to the dorms where they may live. Mikey figures this will be a great practice for his new job. When he starts driving a trolley around downtown Dallas. Which is in two weeks.

The first part of the morning is pretty mundane. Just driving around, and around campus in a huge circle basically. People get on, people get off. Not much to see. The people are all very friendly though. They seem to really appreciate the ride. Mikey guesses it is better than walking. Because it's probably two miles across this campus.

At lunchtime, he takes a quick break and finds a vending machine. Just as soon he sets down to eat his sandwich, his pager goes off with 911. He dropped his sandwich and rushed back to the transit office. He tells them he has to go to a fire and runs out the door. He is only five or six miles from the firehouse and gets there rather quickly.

As he cranks up the firetruck and pulls out of the firehouse. He hears the dispatcher on the radio saying, "Taylor Trailer Park, South Pine Avenue". Mikey just turns and looks at the guys sitting behind him. He says, "I know that place. I've been there before."

Ten minutes later they pull under an old broken sign that reads, 'Taylor Trailer

Park - Enter at your own Risk'. Mikey can see the smoke just barreling out of a trailer on the far right-hand side of the park. He drives the truck over as fast as he can. He grabbed his gear and he and another guy ran into the burning trailer house. He starts running through the house screaming, FIRE DEPARTMENT!, FIRE DEPARTMENT! as loud as he can.

He doesn't see anybody or hear anything. He runs down the burning hallway and enters the back bedroom. Where he sees a small girl lying in the corner, in the fetal position, not moving. She looks to be maybe five or six years old and she is not breathing. Mikey throws off his mask and quickly starts giving her mouth to mouth resuscitation. He gives her chest compressions as he yells for the other guy to get in the back bedroom.

Just as his partner arrives he starts forcing air into her lungs again. His partner starts chest compressions. Just then the little girl made a coughing, choking noise. Mikey says, "Thank you Jesus", out loud. Just out of instinct, he grabbed the little girl and started running for the front door. With all the smoke he didn't notice a giant hole that had burned through the hallway floor.

Mikey, his partner, and the girl all fell through the floor. His feet landed on the ground under the trailer house. He was standing there in the middle of the hallway, still cradling the little girl. The floor of the trailer was now even with his waist. He had to climb up through burning floorboards, ash, and rubble. Back up onto the living room floor.

He took his fire coat off and wrapped it around the little girl's body. He couldn't see anything in the thick black smoke. He grabbed for anything he could to help pull himself up out of the hole. Finally, in the darkness, he managed to grab the arm of the sofa and pull himself up out of the hole. Then he made a mad dash for the front door, with the other guy following him.

He handed the wrapped up girl to the paramedics who were already waiting in the street. He then sat down on the adjacent trailers' front porch to catch his breath. Just then he watched as the entire roof collapsed into itself on the burning trailer he had just run out of. He sat there for about ten minutes and watched that burning trailer turn to ashes right before his eyes. They didn't even try to put it out. It was already gone.

Mikey was sitting there with his head down trying to digest what had just happened. When a hand reached down in front of him as if to shake his hand. He looked up to see Magill with tears running down his face. Magill said, "Man, that's my baby sister Reli you just pulled out of that fire". Mikey reached up, shook Magill's hand and said, "Is she going to be okay"?

Magill said, "She inhaled a lot of smoke and is having trouble breathing. They are going to transport her to the hospital and monitor her overnight. She has a bad burn on her leg. But thanks to you, she is still alive. My mother is in the ambulance with her, she is going to the hospital to watch over Reli. I told them I would be there as soon as I can get a ride to the hospital". Mikey looked at him and smiled. He said, "You want to ride in a Firetruck"? Magill said, "Sure man, thank you. But first I gotta show you something, follow me".

Mikey followed Magill four trailers to the right. They went inside and walked to the bedroom. Magill pointed to a metal footlocker beside the bed and said, "Open it". Mikey walked over to the box and pulled open the lid. On one side was a shotgun, a handgun and two boxes of shells. On the other side was about every hand tool and jack you could imagine ever needing on a tow truck. Underneath the hand tools were chains and hooks and tie-down straps and bungee cords.

On the inside of the metal lid, there was a brand new, (shiny), set of magnetic tow lights. Mikey just sat there on his knees and exhaled a really deep breath. He looked up at Magill and said, "Thank you". Magill said, "The $200 is long gone and I sold the CB radio, but everything else is there. I will pay you back for the cash and radio". Mikey said, "Grab that end and help me put this box in the back seat of the firetruck".

After they got the container into the back of the firetruck. Mikey gave Magill a ride to the hospital. On the way, Mikey told Magill about his ideas to clean up the trailer park. He said he could borrow a couple of dump trucks and a tractor and they could start hauling off all the old junk cars. He said if Magill would help him and maybe get a couple of more volunteers from the trailer park. They could make pretty quick work of it. He said after they got all of the junk picked up, he would borrow a brush hog and mow the entire place.

He told Magill they could take the money from all the junk cars and scrap metal, clear a spot behind the trailer park and build an actual playground for the kids with swings and slides. He said, "If there is any money left, I have another idea also". Magill said, "Man that would be awesome. This place has looked like a dump my whole life. I will get everybody to help us". He said, "No one has ever mowed or cleaned up anything around here. I think people gave up trying a long time ago. And now they don't even seem to care".

Mikey smiled and reached across the seat and shook Magill's hand. He said, "It's a deal then. We start in the morning." They made it to the hospital and checked on Reli. The doctor said she would be fine in a few days. They just needed to clear her lungs because she had breathed in a lot of smoke. They even said her burned leg should heal up nicely.

======================

After dropping Magill at the hospital and checking on Reli. Mikey drives the firetruck straight to O'malley's Towing Service. He walked in and told supervisor Joe to come outside. He says, "I got a present for you, Joe. I know it's not Christmas time yet, but come look". Joe walks outside and says, "Thanks Mikey, you got me a firetruck"? Mikey smiled and asked him to grab one end of the giant box and help him get it out of the back of the firetruck. They pulled the box out and Mikey opened it.

Joe's face lit up with a big smile. He said, "Where the heck did you find this"? Mikey said, "It's a long story Joe, but it's all in there except the $200 in cash and the CB radio. Joe said, "Well that's great Mike, I believe you have already paid me more than enough to cover the $200 and the radio. How about we just call it even"?

Mikey again sighed and let out a deep breath of air. He said, "That would be just great Joe, Thank you, Sir". Joe said, "You're a good man Mike, It's hard to find a good and honest man these days, but you are a good man Mike".

Mikey returned the fire truck to the firehouse. With a huge weight lifted off his shoulders. He called the transit office at the University of North Texas at Dallas. He thanked them for the job. Then said he wouldn't be returning today or any other day.

Then he called Ted at Part-Time Driver and also thanked him for the job for the past twelve years. He said, " Ted, you have been like a father figure to me and I really appreciate everything you have done for me over the years". He said he would come by on Friday and shake Ted's hand and get his final paycheck. But he explained to Ted how he had something else he needed to do for the next week before starting his new job with the city. He told Ted he was going to help the residents clean up Taylor's Trailer Park. He said,

"Thank you for everything Ted, you have been a very good friend to me".

After he got off the phone with Ted. He called the mayor's office. After being transferred by the secretary. He said, "Hello Mr. Mayor, this is Michael Van Winkel. How are you today Sir"? The mayor said, "Well Howdy Mike, how the heck are ya"? Mikey said, "I am going to take that new job with the city in about two weeks. Thank you, Sir, for offering it. I will make you proud."

Then he explained his entire plan to the mayor. He told him how he planned to spend the next week helping the residents of Taylor Trailer Park clean the whole place up. He said he was going to haul off all the trash and junk cars. Then he was going to mow all the high grass and clear an area in the back for a playground. He planned to do some painting and even put up a new sign.

The mayor said, "That would be great Mike. That place has been an eyesore for the city for a very long time. Is there anything I can do to help"? Mikey said, "Yes Sir, I need you to deliver two or three large trash dumpsters out there first thing in the morning. I will take it from there." The mayor said, "No problem Mike, I will get it done. Thank you for all your hard work, congratulations on the new job". Mikey said, "Thank you, sir".

After that, he called Bob at Hoopers Construction. He told Bob all of his plans to clean up the trailer park. He asked Bob if he could borrow two dump trucks and a front end loader. Bob said, "You know Mike, you have been a good worker for me for many years. I really appreciate the good jobs you have helped me complete over the years. You can borrow anything you need to. And by the way, congratulations! on your new job." Mikey said, "Thank you, Bob. I will be out early in the morning to get the trucks".

With that, he hung up and called Maria at her office. He said, "Hey girly, I miss you. How's your day going?" She said, "Great, just shuffling paperwork. How are you, sweetie?" He told her it had been a long day. Then he told her his plan to clean up the trailer park. He said he had help coming from Bob at Hooper's and even the mayor was pitching in some help. She said, "That's great Mikey, I'm so proud of you. You are such a sweet man. I'm a lucky girl."

She said, "We'll see you about supper time then?" He said, "Yes, ma'am. I love you, baby".

Then he figured he had everything arranged for tomorrow, as best he could. So he went home for a shower and a nap. Later that evening he went to Maria's house for a wonderful dinner and a couple of hours of playing with the kids. Where he ended up spending the night again...

Chapter Eighteen
<u>New Park</u>

Early the next morning Mikey went to the Taylor Trailer Park to get Magill. As soon as he pulled in, he could see a difference. There were three big city trash dumpsters by the front gate. Just about every able-bodied resident was throwing trash and debris into those dumpsters. Magill was out there directing everything. Mikey walked up to Magill and said," How's Reli doing"? Magill said, "Ask her yourself, she is right over there. They let her out early this morning". Mikey just smiled.

He told Magill he needed him to help go get the two dump trucks and front end loader. Bob at Hoopers Construction had loaned them. He asked Magill if he knew how to drive a dump truck. Magill said he could drive a stick shift car, but he had never driven a truck before. Mikey said, "That's close enough, I'm about to give you a crash course".

When they got to Mikey's car, Magill said, "before we go there is something I need to say". He told Mikey he was sorry for everything. He said he was sorry for stealing the tools and stuff from the truck. But mostly he was sorry for the way he had treated Mikey and the way he had acted towards him.

He told him that ever since his dad had passed away he had been getting worse and worse. Slipping farther and farther into gang violence and peer pressure. He said he hated himself for the way he had been acting for the past few years. He said he was going to turn his life around and get a (real) job to help his mother and sister. He said he was done with gangs and bad people. He wanted a better life for him and his family.

Mikey said, "Today we take the first step, brother. We're going to clean this place up and make it a respectable place to live. Those gang bangers won't even want to hang out here anymore. With a little hard work, this place will look as good as new". Then he reached out and shook Magill's hand. He said, "Apology accepted, Sir".

When they got to Hooper's, Mikey spent about 30 minutes showing Magill how to drive, shift and maneuver a dump truck before they left the yard. He was surprised how quickly Magill understood everything he said. After a few short lessons, Magill was handling it like a pro. Mikey drove the big dump truck pulling a trailer with a front end loader on it. Magill followed in another dump truck.

Back at Taylor's they quickly got to work. They used the front end loader to crush six junk cars and loaded them into the largest dump truck. Then they loaded all the scrap metal into the other dump truck. Old appliances, bicycle parts, and lawnmowers. Anything made out of metal that they could recycle and get money for, they loaded it all up.

Then Magill followed Mikey to the recycling scale. After unloading both trucks and weighing out. They went inside together to get paid. They got just over $1100. The next morning they did the whole thing all over again. They loaded both dump trucks with the scrap metal from the trailer house that had burnt and two others that had fallen down years before. This trip to the scale rewarded them with another $650, for a total of just over $1750 from all the scrap metal, they were able to recycle.

Mikey said, "Guess what we are going to do with this money"? Magill said, "What". He said, "We are going to clear an area behind the trailer park and put in a playground for the kids. Then we are going to put in a basketball court." Magill said, "Sweet everyone will love that".

The following day Mikey brush hogged all the grass at the trailer park. By dark, it looked like a manicured garden. The next day he cleared an area behind the trailer park. He used the front end loader to level out the ground and smooth the whole area out. Mikey, Magill and several men from the trailer park set up two by four forms. 100 feet long and 20 feet wide. For a concrete pad, that would be a basketball court.

The next morning Mikey pulled into Taylor's with a concrete mixer full of concrete. He borrowed the truck from Mccormack Ready Mix. And paid for the concrete out of the $1750 scrap metal money. He will need 25 yards of concrete to fill the 100ft by 20ft pad. His truck can only haul nine yards at a time. So Mikey will have to make three trips today. Back and forth between the concrete plant and the basketball court.

Mikey lets Magill drive the concrete mixer all day with him in the passenger seat showing him what to do. He shows Magill how to properly back the truck, and use his mirrors to find blind spots. He shows him how to operate the drum, turning it forward and backward. He teaches him how to load and unload the chutes. He shows him how to rinse the drum after every load so the old concrete doesn't set up in the drum.

He shows him how to check the tires and take the slack out of the slack adjuster on his brake chambers. He shows him how to check, use and fill the water tanks. He teaches him everything he knows about (slump) and the different ways to mix a load of concrete. He shows him how to check the fluid levels, lights, and fuel evaporator pop-off valve on the truck. That day Mikey teaches Magill everything he knows about operating a concrete mixer in the real world. He shows him what to do, what not to do, and what to watch out for.

====================

The concrete cost $60 a yard. So this 25 yards of concrete will cost about $1500. Mikey had the concrete plant add sky blue die to the loads of concrete. By the end of the day, they have the only sky blue basketball court anybody has ever seen. It's absolutely beautiful. Mikey shakes hands with all the residents who pitched in and help him with the spreading out and finishing of the concrete pad. He tells them all that he is proud of the job they have done. It looks awesome.

Everybody including Mikey and Magill wrote their names on the edge of the wet concrete. Two days later after setting a pole with a backboard at each end. They all played the first-ever game of basketball at Taylors Trailer Park. Then Mikey handed Magill a brand new sign he had made for the front gate. It says, "Taylor's Acres" in a beautiful sky blue color. Magill, with his chest sticking out a foot, proudly hangs it above the main gate.

Mikey said, "I spent the last of the $1750 on that sign. We are out of money.

I'm going to talk to the mayor in the morning about giving us a grant from the city for $2500 to put swings and slides in our new playground area". Magill said, "Good luck on that one buddy".

===================

The day they finished pouring the concrete pad Mikey had let Magill drive the concrete truck back to Mccormick Ready Mix. Mr. Mccormick met them at the front gate. He said, "I have been watching you guys coming in and out all day". He said, "What's your name son"? Magill shook his hand and said. "Magill Sir". Mr. Mccormick said, "You handle that truck pretty good. You want a job"? Magill looked at Mikey, (who was smiling like a Cheshire cat), then he looked back at Mr. Mccormick and said, "Hell Yes - Sir".

Mr. Mccormick said, "Well you had a good teacher there. You start on Monday, at seven o'clock sharp!" Then Mr. Mccormick winked at Mikey and walked away. Magill looked at Mikey and said, "You have been planning this all day haven't you"? Mikey said, "No Sir, I have been planning it all week". Magill gave Mikey a big hug and said, "You are the man Mikey, You the man. Thank you."

Mikey knew they still had a lot of work to get done at Taylor's. He told Magill to go home and get some rest, and he did the same. He was exhausted but felt very proud of what they had already accomplished. And he looked forward to finishing the job. He had always prided himself in seeing a project through to the end. Another good lesson he had learned from his father. He couldn't wait to see the finished playground. And watch the kids enjoying it.

Chapter Nineteen
<u>Happy Endings</u>

The next morning, Mikey was standing in front of the mayor's office when he opened the front door. He asked the mayor to take a ride with him out to Taylors Trailer Park to have a look around. The mayor agreed, and on the ride out Mikey explained what he had in mind. He told the mayor how he needed a $2500 grant from the city of Dallas. To put playground equipment at the site where he had cleared and leveled the ground behind the trailer park.

He explained how they had hauled off all the junk and trash. How they had mowed and cleaned the entire trailer park. How they had even poured concrete with the recycling money and built a basketball court. After a quick tour through the trailer park, the mayor was impressed with all the work they had done.

The mayor said here is what I will do. I will have Community Action Service donate all the playground equipment you need. If you will let me tell the city council that this whole project was my idea. He said the city council has been against me for the past year. This will give me favor with them, and I will get a lot of votes next year when I run for re-election because of this project.

He said, "Tomorrow I will have all the playground equipment delivered here to this site. Then, two or three days after that we will have a ribbon-cutting ceremony right here and invite the whole city. News camera crews and everything. Mikey said, "Okay if that's what it takes to get the equipment for the kids then let's do it".

=====================

The next morning Magill called Mikey and said, "You better hurry up and get over here man". When Mikey pulled into "Taylor's Acres", there were two flatbed trailers loaded with (Swing-n-Slide) playground equipment parked right in front of the area Mikey had cleared for a playground. The residents were already unloading it and had even started setting it up. There were slides and swing sets and monkey bars and a jungle gym looking thing. With a giant merry-go-round for the center of the playground. They had a tetherball set and a volleyball net.

Mikey looked at Magill and they both smiled at each other. Magill said, "Pretty cool, huh"? Mikey said, "Yeah, that mayor is on the ball. Let's get this stuff set up so the kids can start playing".

It took them all of that day and most of the next to set up all of the playground equipment. About nine a.m. on the third day people started showing up for the ribbon-cutting ceremony. Apparently, the mayor had put out flyers and told the news stations. By noon it looked like the entire city of Dallas was there at Taylor's Acres.

The first people to show up were the entire fire department where Mikey volunteered. They brought all of their smoking gear and cooked hot dogs and chicken strips for everybody. Ted Mulberry, from (Part-Time Driver), and his wife were there. Joe O'Malley from O'Malley's Towing Service was there with his girlfriend. Youth pastor Mark was there with his wife and kids. Mr. Mccormick, from Mccormick's Ready Mix, was also there with his wife.

The entire Carmichael family was there from Carmichael's Trucking. They had brought all of the secretaries and dispatchers that worked for their company. Bob from Hooper's construction was there, with what looked like every truck driver in the Dallas Ft. Worth metroplex. The guy who owned the Checkered Cab Company (whom Mikey had never met) was there, with a van load of taxi drivers. Frank Barnes, from Express Bulls, was even there.

Even Mikey's old football buddy from high school, Bart Jackson and his wife were there. Mikey looked at Bart and said, "What, you couldn't get Mark Cuban to come"? Virtually every member of the congregation at the First Baptist Church of Dallas was there with their families. It was like a city-wide party.

As Mikey and Maria walked through the enormous crowd shaking everybody's hand and saying hello. They spotted Magill and his family setting over by the playground. Mikey wanted to introduce

Maria to Magill so they walked over and said hello. Mikey said, "Magill this is my girlfriend Maria". Magill said, "Hi Maria, You have a really great guy for a boyfriend".

Mikey told Maria he needed to talk to Magill for a minute. He left her by the playground where Charlie and Rosemary were already sliding and swinging. He asked Magill how his first day at Mccormick's Ready Mix had gone.

Magill said, "It was a great day man! I hauled two loads of concrete to a site where they are building a brand new house. Then I hauled two more loads downtown where a sidewalk was under construction. All the people who work at Mccormick's were very nice to me. I had a great day. I can't wait to go back tomorrow. Thank you, Mikey, for everything."

Then he said, "Mr. Mccormack is even paying for night classes so I can go to truck driving school and get my (CDL), Commercial Drivers License". Mikey said, "Wow Magill, that is so great. I am proud of you, keep up the good work. You can have anything you want in this world as long as you are willing to put in the work to get it, so keep up the good work my friend".

Just then someone grabbed Mikey's arm, he turned around to see Detective Williams. Detective Williams said. "Hey Mike, I heard you recovered the stolen items from your vandalized truck". Mikey said, "Yes Sir, I sure did". Williams said, "Well did you find out who the thief was"? Mikey hesitated for a moment, He was looking right at Magill.

He looked back at Detective Williams and said, "No Sir, all I know is an anonymous person left a large box in the back seat of one of our fire trucks. Maybe they felt guilty and are trying to turn their lives around. Even if we find out who did it, I don't want to press charges since everything was recovered". The detective said, "Fair enough Mike. When I get back to the office I will close the case file on this one and move on to more important matters. You fellas have a nice day."

Mikey and Magill looked at each other and smiled. Magill said, "Thanks again buddy, you're awesome, man". Then he said, "Is your girlfriend Latino"? Mikey said,

"Yes, she is from Puerto Rico. Why?" Magill said, "I already had mad respect for you, Mikey because you are the nicest guy I've ever met. But I thought you were just another white guy who grew up on the other side of town. I can't believe you are dating a Latina girl. Props man, serious props." He gave Mikey the thumbs up as he walked away smiling.

=====================

The mayor arrived twenty minutes late and made his grand entrance. He stood on the merry-go-round and cut the red ribbon with a giant pair of scissors. He said, "I want to dedicate this playground to the fine families of 'Taylor's Acres'. This is the first of many projects on my agenda to clean up the south side of Dallas. With your help, and your vote. We will make it happen together". The crowd cheered wildly. Mikey just smiled.

Mikey spent the next two days helping volunteers at Taylors Acres paint the fence that went all the way around the property. When they had finished, the whole trailer park looked like it had been completely revamped. Mikey shook everyone's hands and thanked them for all their help and hard work. He told them if they needed anything not to hesitate to call him.

That weekend Mikey took Maria and the kids to Lake Texoma for an overnight camping and fishing trip. He wanted to get in one more trip with the kids before starting his new job with the city on Monday. They had a blast at the lake fishing and swimming. They even caught a mess of strippers that Mikey and Maria cooked over the campfire for dinner that evening. He told Maria they made a good team and she agreed.

====================

Monday morning Mikey showed up at the trolley station office, where he met his new boss, Mrs. Cook. She showed him around the facilities and told him which trolley he would be driving. After he met the dispatcher Sherel and the two other drivers Herb and Little Ricky. (Little Ricky was about 400 pounds). He went out and completed his pre-trip inspection on his trolley and fired it up. He then went over the map of his route and down the street he went.

Mikey had a great day, that first day on the job. He thought Mrs. Cook and the people he worked with were all really nice folks. He enjoyed driving around the city and meeting all the friendly people he gave a ride to that day. He spent the day just driving around like a normal streetcar. Shuttling people from downtown to the Plaza District and from downtown to the Arts District and from downtown to the Theater and Shopping Districts.

By the end of the day, Mikey had realized that this was right where he belonged. The job was easy going, almost relaxing to him. The people were nice and he felt like he fit right in. He couldn't ask for a better job. He thought it was a pretty good gig for an old truck driver. He gave thanks to God for his life and his new job. He knew he would be able to stay home and have a family now. Instead of being on the road and gone all of the time. He had spent his whole life helping others. Now he felt like it was his turn to be happy.

After work that first day Mikey had a giant smile on his face. Everyone could see how happy he was. He seemed to be almost beaming with a new glow about him. He went straight to Maria's house after work. He knocked on the door and waited. When she opened the door, he was down on one knee holding a small box in the air. The twinkle in her eyes and the Texas-size smile on her face said it all…

The End

From The Author

I have had this story about Mikey in my head for many years. But I had been working on my other two books and never seemed to have time for Mikey. Once I put pen to paper, this story came naturally. It was so easy to write since most of the (Adventures of Mikey's) life are based on my own adventures driving commercial vehicles for more than 25 years. All the characters in this story are people I met while working at different jobs in my life and career.

Det. Williams is an actual detective who helped me many times when I was in the used car business and found several stolen cars. Herb and Little Ricky are actual guys I worked at the trolley station with, many years ago. Bob Hooper was an actual construction man I drove a dump truck for. He was a big-hearted, old school guy and I really liked him. Maria was a beautiful Latina girl I loved in my younger days until she ran away with a guy who spoke her own language.

Taylors Village was an actual trailer park I lived in when my daughter Melissa was little. (You can read all about Melissa in my first book). Mr. Taylor was a great old man who would give the shirt off his back to help a fellow human being. He spent his entire life building that trailer park. When he passed away, the park was willed to his grandson. A guy I went to high school with. The grandson gave everybody who lived there 30 days to get out. Then he came in and bulldozed all the trailer houses down and burned them off. Putting all those families out into the street. Most of which had small children.

Then he put cattle on the land. If you drive by today, you can still see the gas meters sticking out of the ground, marking where each trailer stood. I bet old man Taylor would roll over in his grave if he could see what his grandson did with his life's work. Madness.

I did even once find a poor homeless guy in a used car, just trying to get out of the cold and snow. He really did suffocate from the fumes of his burning charcoal. I did have to stay and fill out a police report.

And Mikey is right. We can all do a little more to help with the homeless crisis in our own neighborhoods. Look in the mirror. I was homeless once and living in my car between jobs before I went to truck driving school. If we all do a little, it would add up to a lot of help for the homeless.

I have driven 18-wheelers cross country, concrete mixers, dump trucks, trolleys and transit buses, even a tow truck and a taxi cab. However I have never driven a Zamboni :) I truly enjoyed writing this story of Mikey's adventures. I can only hope you guys enjoy it as much.

=====================

I want to thank my children. They are my inspiration for living and writing every day. I love you guys.

If you enjoyed this book please leave a brief review on Amazon or Goodreads. Your reviews help other readers find books they may like to read. It also helps the author know if they are writing stuff that people are enjoying. I always love reading the reviews and feedback from my readers. So please take a moment and write a small review. Thank you. God bless you and your family and everything you love.
Happy Reading.

=====================

If you liked reading this book please check out my other books on Amazon and Goodreads. Here are the links.

https://www.amazon.com/dp/B07KY6GFD4

https://www.amazon.com/dp/B07L2CNBFV

https://www.goodreads.com/author/show/17726900.T_J_Wray

T. J. Wray

Follow me to get updates on new books coming out and get signed up for my giveaways. Or to ask me any other questions you may have.

My Twitter Page:
https://twitter.com/TJamesWray

My Website:
https://sites.google.com/view/tjwray/home

My Goodreads Author Page:
https://www.goodreads.com/author/show/17726900.T_J_Wray

www.ingramcontent.com/pod-product-compliance
Lightning Source LLC
Chambersburg PA
CBHW070953120726
47910CB00004B/1215